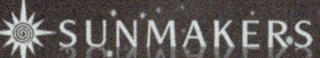

SUNMAKERS

SECRETS of OXFORD

Aura Willow

Text ©2014 Aura Willow

Secrets of Oxford

Published by Sunmakers, a division of Eldamar Ltd,
157 Oxford Road, Cowley, Oxford, OX4 2ES, UK
www.sunmakers.co.uk
Tel +44(0)1865 779944

Version 1.0

Cover design and typography by Ayd Instone.
Edited by Rachel Instone www.sunmakers.co.uk

Cover image incorporates the images: Portraits of a beautiful goth girl by
Sergei Kleshnev via 123rf.com and Bridge of Sighs connecting Hertford
College and New College Lane in Oxford by LanceB via istockphoto.com.

ISBN: 978-1-908693-22-8

www.thesecretsofoxford.blogspot.co.uk

I dedicate this book to everyone who has ever believed in me and my eccentricity, and of course to Oxford Alae.

I would like to say a huge thank you to the brilliant Rachel and Ayd Instone for making this possible. A further thanks to my editors Rachel Instone and Jessie Carr for being brave enough to read this stuff first and then helping to make it sparkle.

Thank you also to my hubby, my girls and my parents for being amazing, and to all my friends and family who have supported me, too many to mention (and I'd hate to forget anyone), you know who you are.

In memory of my Grandma and my English teacher Mr Clifford who both had faith in me.

Keep smiling.

"We live, we love and we continue to rise, as/like angels watching over all and everyone."

Contents

Bad Angel 7

Astral Walker 43

Death from Dreaming Spires 73

Him 101

Guide 147

Ghouls of Grandpont 175

Demon Decoy Transport Trauma 193

Beware of the Gnomes 209

Indigenous 225

The Phantom of Oxford 247

About the Author 302

Bad Angel

February 2005

I had nothing back home, nothing worth holding on to anyway. It was time to move on from Abingdon where everybody knew your name, reported your business. I could do without that. Oxford had always had a place in my heart; it was like going from school to college, like growing up. I was ready now, more than ready, to move on, to find my own feet. I would start with a new identity, change my name, age, and look, be someone new. I didn't want to be bad, just do something completely other than 'reliable'. No more reliability, I was going to be unpredictable to all who already knew me and find a new crowd. A big city stood before me as I stepped majestically off the bus, like a warrior dismounting her stallion before royalty, a kid stepping into a sweet shop. Sensations of fear, excitement and doubt coursed through my blood with just a step off the bus. It was now or never to take this step, to be bold. My torn Converse took care of my doubt and marched forward.

Where could I go? Anywhere, with limitations. What could I do? Anything, with limitations. What were the limitations? Everything other than the streets. The streets were limitless and dangerous. Locks, gates and walls would protect things from the street, but the paths and alleyways would take me around the city to see the truths, lies and secrets concealed in the stone.

I spent a couple of weeks in my element figuring out shortcuts, regular faces, the routines of the city goers. I was a living map. The long black coat I wore defined me; I was a shadow, watching, like the gargoyles. I seemed to be recognised by only a few, the few who were also shadows, intentionally ignored, the guys on the street. Some weren't so friendly; we noticed each other but exchanged warning vibes. Others started to smile as we passed one another and eventually I realised that perhaps this was the crowd I was to become a part of. Something flagged up from long ago that instead of giving money it was more acceptable to offer food or drinks, I had never asked why. At the time I was told this, the world was all sparkles and rainbows; I had accepted that it must be a more honourable gift to those in need. So I began to introduce myself to regular faces, offering them coffee. I began to feel wanted, appreciated. This wasn't high school where I was the walked over dirt, I was a heroine. Then one day I came across Ash.

He was one of them, making his living on the street, but he was tidy. He glowed; tall, pale, slick hair and hypnotising eyes. He wore a tight, black t-shirt and jeans, flashing off a smart belt and Doc Marten boots. He looked pure but dressed like a rock icon: devilish.

August 2005

There hadn't been a day since February that I hadn't seen Ash. I idolised him, everything he said, and everything he did. I was in love with him. There was no way I could admit this though, no way. He was too cool, too smooth to be in love with anyone and especially me. Tonight though we were going to some party he had heard about. With any luck the alcohol would take over and things would happen. I'd stayed clean of drugs until now, if there was one thing I'd promised myself it was that I would not fall into that trap. Some promises had to be broken though, especially now, and even if only for one night.

I walked through St Giles deep in thought, crazed in my fantasy. Music blasted through my headphones and the sun blinded my sight as I attempted to cross the busy road.

The last couple of moments of my life whizzed before my eyes... The speeding police car approached me aggressively, its sirens blaring. The car it was chasing had swerved in to the next lane, over-taking a bus, unable to brake. I felt myself being propelled from the ground, powerless to resist. Then came the inevitable end, I felt my neck snap as my body fell awkwardly to the ground. The darkness was upon me.

Not for long though. The light soon returned I had been wrong, I was ok! I stood up in relief. The relief was only temporary however as I turned to see my wasted life lying sprawled on the ground, outlined by a pool of blood, as people screamed looking at it. The worst thing was, Ash would never know.

"I hear that this is the worst part," I heard a female voice say behind me.

"Excuse me?" I questioned, turning to see what appeared to be an angel standing next to me. Her hair was long and brown, her wings were white and she wore a long, luxurious purple crushed velvet gown.

"I have always been an angel, Zena, though you have a different path. Not many angels are chosen from the human race, but the Higher Powers have many plans for you. From what I have heard this part must be a little surreal, looking down at your own dead body," she said.

"Right," I acknowledged as I watched the paramedics attending to me, then eventually giving up and zipping my body into a black body bag.

"I am Emma by the way, your guardian, shall we say. So this is the part where you normally have a choice: to fall asleep eternally and move on to the next world, or you can vow to help those who are dying in the city to die peacefully."

"You said 'normally have a choice'. Forgive me for thinking I don't?" I turned to her with a cranky expression.

"No one is denying you a choice, Zena, but there is great hope for you," she said gently.

"Yeah you already mentioned that, and I prefer to be called 'Zen' actually if you don't mind. Ok, so sell it to me then, why should I stick around?" I said defensively still a little bewildered that I was talking to a beautiful woman with huge wings, apparently invisible to the world.

"Well for starters, I know how much you love this city and Ash, for instance ... In your free time you are permitted to wander earth. You can still be with him, in a sense. And think of how many people you could help. The best bit is you get to learn of all the secrets in the world," she persuaded.

Ash. I thought, I would get to see Ash. My cocky defence dropped, I could use this opportunity to help him.

"I'll do it," I said, urgently now.

"I'm glad to hear it," she gave me a warm hug. The city around us faded.

June 2010

I knew more than I could ever have wished to know. I had learnt of the reality that vampires, demons, werewolves, ghosts, witches, demi-gods, and many more beings walked the earth. The Gods and Goddesses, otherwise known as the Higher Powers, were real; living in a realm above, below and in Earth that I was not yet permitted to access. I had helped many people of Oxford cross the barrier between life and death by gently comforting them and taking their hand to walk over the threshold.

I was still me, though I had the black wings of a human chosen angel, and they were kind of handy when persuading people that there would be an afterlife waiting for them. It wasn't for me forever though. I had to get back to Ash; just looking upon him forever wasn't good enough. I knew what to do. I'd already had a few warnings for interfering with his fate. The Higher Powers apparently didn't like me guiding him away from danger, and in turn inflicting it on the people that would dare to betray his friendship.

I was on my last warning; if I was to interfere one more time then I would fall. This meant I would return to the cruel earth, knowing its secrets, still carrying angelic blood but with no powers.

I waited for him to return home, knowing the drugs he would inject into his bloodstream would be too strong to survive. I had played the sweet innocent game to my supervisors who allowed me to stay by his side when the time came whilst his angel came to take him. It wasn't long before he was supposed to die. I wouldn't have to conceal this knife much longer.

He injected his poison and there as he drifted to sleep appeared his angel. 'A tall, white winged, muscular male angel. It would be harder to kill him than I had hoped. Of course the Higher Powers knew I would try something'. I thought to myself.

"Zena," he greeted me.

"Hello," I replied coldly.

"Do you want to say good bye?" the male angel asked me.

"No, I just want to be here," I lied, standing back so as not to look like a threat to his work.

As the angel concentrated on gaining Ash's attention, I lunged at him, my knife sliced his shoulder. I had originally planned to kill the angel, but earlier it seemed my luck had changed...

* * *

"Zena, my name is Silas. I've been given the job to escort Ash. As you know, he is destined to be taken soon." The angel approached me as I wandered the city.

I nodded.

"There are prophecies, Zena, things I have heard that entwine your fate with Ash's. I want to help you but you must listen carefully. The Higher Powers are going to be watching you very carefully, perhaps even tapping into your thoughts. When I come to take Ash you must think as if we have not met, in fact act surprised that I am a male, and then you attack me, you understand?"

"I do, but why do you want to help me?" I wondered.

"Because I fell in love with a human once, but there was nothing I could do to prevent her dying. I don't want you to go through the same. You fight for him, do it for the both of us. If I can prevent your loss then my wounds may feel a little less sore," Silas prompted.

I smiled sadly. "What will I do though? He'll go straight to the underworld if there is no angel to guide him."

"You inject this into him, this is an antidote, and he will live," Silas handed me a syringe.

"And what about when I fall, how will I survive?" I wondered.

"You make your way to Pembroke Street before you fall; you will have time before the Higher Powers call upon you, but not much," he answered.

"And what happens at Pembroke Street?" I asked.

"You will be met by a vampire, a friend, who has been briefed by me. You will become the first vampiric angel, and your new fate will begin," Silas smiled reassuringly.

"Silas, thank you," I said, humbled by his generosity.

"Oh Zena, just one more thing," he said. "Some time, far in the future someone you know will have to confront you. Remember this and how you have had to confront me to protect who you love."

"I don't follow."

"Let's just say, you might meet Emma in your new life. The words she will speak do not necessarily convey how she truly feels."

"Ok," I replied, still very confused. "Silas, may I ask how you know this?"

"Not all the Higher Powers agree with each other, someone's always got your back kid," he smiled once more before disappearing.

* * *

I felt awful about hurting Silas, but it had to be done or he would be found out for helping me and I would lose Ash.

Not losing any time I pulled the syringe from my pocket and injected the antidote into Ash's vein. His eyes opened as if nothing had happened. I took his hand invisibly for a second before I left for Pembroke Street.

Sure enough I was greeted by the vampire Silas had told me about. If it hadn't been for my angelic senses I wouldn't have recognised him, his face was just like any human's.

"Are you Zena?" he asked.

"I prefer 'Zen', but yes that's me," I replied.

"We haven't much time before you officially fall. Come here."

Without hesitation he secured my neck with his hands then exposed his fangs and punctured my vein. The venom trickled through me like fire. I gave in to the pain and passed out.

"When you wake you will be new," he said and left my body slumped over the steps of a house, transforming into a new being.

When I woke I left the city, just for a couple of months, just to cope with the change. Just until I was ready to face Ash again in person.

September 2011

I'm not sure what happened to the time. I never forgot about Ash. I saw him occasionally as I passed through the shadows of Oxford; pretending not to care. His poison had started to take a toll on his look but he was still angelic to me. The beautiful moments we had shared never escaped my memory. There were plenty of occasions we had spent afternoons together, sat on a wall in town, he'd drink, and I'd pretend to smoke. He'd invited me to join his habit but somehow I'd found the strength to decline politely and tried to hold onto him soberly. He'd never known what had happened to me. Never would, not until I confided in him. I expect he thought my life had taken another direction, maybe he never did wonder. Five years dead, a long time to think, but now I was back. Dead girl walking, just like him, except he was a ticking time bomb, I had eternity. I had a slightly different look now. I was aged or matured rather; slightly fleshier than the slender bones I was once. At first I hated it; a cannibal was what I was; though a choice didn't exist. Not like his habit. He had a choice, it would be hard to overcome but he could live. My drug could not be overcome. As much as I had despised it, blood was my oxygen. The beautiful thing of it now, however, was my need became delectable. Nothing could stop me, I had no qualms about tasting his drug now; it could not hurt me for I had completed my transition. I was whole and about to save him from his harsh fate.

It had been a long time, I didn't know exactly where I could find him, how he would react to seeing me again. I was limited to the shadows too. Confidence wasn't an issue, just where to start. 'Hey Ash, so how've you been? I've been turned into a parasitic angel. Well that's the long and short of it anyway.' Yeah, that would do it, make him think I'd lost my mind.

"Zen?" I heard my name.

There he stood. The sun shone on his face glowing, as I stood sheltering in the dark reflection of University College.

His presence paralysed me.

June 2013

Two years have gone and he still has no idea what has happened to me, he didn't even know he was destroying me through his ignorance. I wanted to tell him everything but he would never believe me. If anything I'd only lose the little attention I occasionally had from him. I had to suffer in silence. It was hard to find time to see him, the sun was an issue, he was able to be both diurnal and nocturnal whereas I was limited to the shadows. Our communication had been mainly through letters. I paid a trusted shopkeeper in town to receive my post as Ash never had any credit on his phone. I would try and find convenient opportunities to ring him between his daily struggles to make a raise. He just assumed I was depressed but never knew the reason why. Then one day I picked up a letter. It was a reply to the last one I'd sent him. When I wrote last I had explained that I'd spent two whole years of trying to drop a hint about my feelings and now finally I had started to accept that we were two very different beings, two life forms that could only ever be friends. I told him that I'd given up on hinting about my feelings but I still cared and I missed him. I reminded him that time hadn't mattered to him once. A long time ago we would spend hours together, but now I mostly saw him in my memories and thoughts. It seemed he thought I was writing him a love letter. In his reply he said he wondered about my feelings for him and that as far as he was concerned we were ok just as friends. His letter left me angry; foolishly I let my human emotions take over. I had thought I was his only friend, his strength; I had let him slowly weaken the supernatural power that possessed me. In return, when eventually he would learn my secret, I thought that he would crave me, beg me to run away with him, beseech me to change him so we could live together eternally. Now I doubted that anything he ever learnt about me would change his mind. Instead he was happy, steady as we were with minimum communication. How wrong he was. He was about to find out that we were definitely not ok.

July 2013

I approached the city ready to take a breath as I thrust up to the surface of this drowning mess I had got myself into. Sticking to the shelter of the college building's shady perimeters I pushed my dark glasses up onto the bridge of my nose and marched in time to the rhythm of Bowie's new album playing on my iPod. Who knew how long I would be marching around looking for him. I knew his regular hang-outs but luck hadn't really been on my side of late. I considered shady routes to travel around the city. As I had evolved from a fallen angel I was fortunate enough to not be full vampire, which gave me the advantage of walking in the day as long as I wasn't in the sun's direct light. I recognised a few faces from long ago but fortunately they didn't recognise me. It was curious Ash had recognised me a couple of years previous. He was then as beautiful as he had always been even if slightly degraded from the drugs. Most recently he looked ill, still pure enough to me, his spirit shone through nevertheless; a twinkle in his eyes and a nice laugh. I had now managed to get myself into the Covered Market sheltering between groups of Oriental tourists who delicately used parasols. I would try and work my way up Market Street and somehow onto Cornmarket Street, that would be difficult. I peered out from the last aisle of the Covered Market looking to my left, no idea how I would avoid self-combustion from the rays of sunlight. Perhaps I could make a dash and seek protection from the phone box. I looked over. Typical – there was someone in it. I had no time for this; I'd have to run in and push them out. I pulled out my ear-plugs and broke into an easy sprint, trying to avoid my skin smoking from too much of the sun's exposure. Opening the door I yelled, "So sorry sir, it's an emergency, I have to use the phone." I looked up at the startled stranger as I finished my sentence. There stood Ash.

"Zen? Hey, are you alright?" he asked in his soothing voice.

This was awkward. He waited for an answer as I suffered a mental panic attack. I had ventured out to better the situation following my last overreaction, instead I had done exactly what I always did where he was concerned; screwed it up even more. My lie excused me from words temporarily as I searched for an answer.

"You need the phone?" he queried.

"No, I needed the phone box, but actually don't anymore. I was, on my way somewhere." I took my shades from my eyes.

"Oh ok," he said casually, which kind of wound me up, I didn't have the words to answer his questions, but his disinterest in my emergency angered me. "Do you mind if I use the phone?" he continued.

"Sure, go ahead," I said.

He waited for me to leave the small space we were sharing.

"I can't leave Ash."

"Ok, well, I'll go to another, I'll see you around," he placed his hand on the door.

"No, Ash don't go, I was looking for you!"

He looked at me with a slightly annoyed expression.

"What's going on with you Zen?"

"I have, some problems, and I really need to speak to you. You've been so distant, and we have a massive lack of communication going on, or an unfortunate chain of misunderstandings."

"Well don't worry, we're cool, ok?"

"No it's not ok. I miss you."

He looked uncomfortable. "So, what've you been up to?"

"Too much to explain in a phone box; although it's good being close to you again."

If he was uncomfortable before, he was now shifty.

"Ash, please just give me a hug," I said in an unintentionally, but extremely successful way of worsening the situation.

To my surprise he did. Despite all my powers, my strength and natural abilities of defence his arms made me feel utterly and completely safe.

"You're so cold," he noticed, leaning away but still embracing me.

"Yeah, I told you I needed to speak to you, but you won't believe what I'm going to tell you, I've, well, I had a series of unfortunate accidents and," I considered whether this was the best time to provide a truthful but incomprehensible explanation, "I fell ill, and I can't be in direct sunlight, I also have trouble controlling my body temperature. I came to find you because we were close once, and the last couple of years it's as if we're strangers when we meet. I need you Ash, I need the same kind of friendship we once had."

"Zen, I can't even look after myself, let alone a friend."

"I'll look out for you Ash, if you lend me an ear and your arms a little more often."

"I was just going to score," he said. He released his arms.

"I kind of figured that. Look, I can help with your habit." I pulled out a twenty from my pocket, one I'd collected from the pocket of my lunch. I handed it to him. "There's more where that came from. And I have a place to stay, much nicer than where you are I'd bet."

His drug-orientated mind ticked, if there had been

any awkwardness before, promises of riches counteracted it.

"Sound," he said. "So do you want to come with me now?"

I smiled. "Yeah, it will be like old times, except I'm much more fun now, we'll get a beer when you're sorted and catch up properly."

Now I was in control. In control of where I wanted this to go, his health and habit and eventually his life...

August 2013

There was a contrast of light in the maisonette over the newsagent I had temporarily taken over. The rain-clouds outside darkened the streets, the bright electric light created a cosy atmosphere contrasted against the damp dull streets outside. Through the small gap in the curtains the windows painted a picture of rain drops peering in at Ash and me. It was daytime, five pm to be precise. Ash had fallen asleep on the sofa. It seemed it was taking him a while to get used to his new surroundings and his new life with me. Still injecting himself with fragments of death, he would come and go a few times a day. I funded his venom with riches picked from a menu of prosperous loners. I had persuaded him to believe that I had inherited it all. Deep down I suspected he questioned why I could not be directly exposed to the sun, but his infected mind decided a funded habit and reliable place to stay were adequate to override that curiosity. We'd had some good times talking and watching movies, but it wasn't what I wanted. I wanted to save his life by taking his soul. I thought if we could become close enough then I could turn him, but we only had a friendship, something I had once doubted would even develop as it had. Whenever I hinted at even slight affection he brushed it off or changed the subject. If I were to wait I could be robbed of the chance, each time I gave him cash for his gear I was handing him a raffle ticket to end his life, eternally. If he drifted away I could not resuscitate him, because of the slight problem of lack of breath. I peered over at his chest, it was still moving up and down rhythmically. I could turn him now. All I had to do was bite him and he would be safe, not only that, he would be besotted with me. It was inevitable when sired by a vampire, with the exception of my siring, the small point that my blood was angelic at the time. I stood up quietly and moved to kneel at his side. His neck was exposed, I craved his blood, craved it as much as his kiss. I placed my hand on the sofa for balance and slowly worked my way towards his vein. I could feel the pain where my heart once was, where it would have been beating, I felt my stomach drop as nerves took over me. I was made a hunter but this guy was a natural antidote to my killing instinct. I hesitated; my body was confusing me, conflicted between human feelings and vampiric cravings. His eyes opened. Quick thinking was completely necessary.

"I'm so sorry Ash, did I wake you? I was trying to find my keys; I was just going to nip out. I thought perhaps they'd fallen under here." I surprised myself with the fluency of my lies and stood up quickly to look somewhere else for my 'lost keys'.

He rubbed the back of his hand across his eyes, and sat up.

"Where were you going Zen? Anywhere nice?" he said, sleepily adjusting his eyes to the light.

"Not really sure, just a walk I guess," I replied.

"Maybe I could come," he queried, I turned around as I looked behind a plant pot. His eyes were optimistic, too polite to ask outright for cash. He smiled whilst waiting for my reply.

"Sure. Let me know where we need to go, I'll get my shoes on." I thought at least we'd get some time together.

I casually walked into one of the two small bedrooms and picked up my army boots to save spoiling the evening walk with soaked through Converse. I heard him talking briefly as I sat on the bed to tie the laces.

I felt his presence in the doorway behind me. "Friars Wharf, forty five minutes?" he said.

"Cool." My trail of thoughts distracted me from noticing that he had walked in and sat next to me.

"You seem distant."

"Sorry, I guess I have a lot on my mind." That wasn't a lie.

"Care to share?" he asked.

"Maybe later. Wouldn't want to push my luck."

He didn't say anything. I guessed he took it as a hint at discussing my feelings toward him.

"I'll be ready in a minute; we can get the bus if you like?" I changed the subject and admitted defeat. What were the chances he would be glad to hear me say that I was jealous of every girl he glanced at when out, that I would rather die again than hear him ask about my old friends now and then. Did he know how much it hurt when I had dedicated my life to protect him and he seemed to go out of his way to make me feel like the most unlovable and unattractive being in the world, and show affections for everyone but me? I had died twice, I had a liquid diet and issues with daytime. I was in love with the most handsome man in the world, a beauty; I could not help being the beast.

"If I'm in the way, Zen, just say. I can move on." He broke my trance.

"I'm the one in the way Ash, you've never understood what I'm about because you haven't taken the time until now to ask, probably out of guilt. I'm going to go out on my own, I'll put some cash in your room." I was wound up from my frustration. I chucked a wad of cash from my pocket into the doorway of his room and slammed the front door. Turned out I didn't know where my keys were, I didn't care, I'd had enough, maybe I was better lonely. I walked the streets, this time able to access the once inaccessible walls of the city. The walls could keep out human scum but not folk like me, I was an angry bad angel. He'd be happy now, with the flat to himself. I wouldn't be a burden to him, he would be able to live his life until he took too much and ended it.

Plenty of opportunities passed with the hours, the rain scattered the crowds into a few lone people. The Old Tom bell struck eleven pm. I ventured down Brasenose Lane.

"There you are!" I heard his voice shouting.

I turned to see him, he looked striking, the street light on his face, the Radcliffe Camera behind him. His hair was dripping, his clothes soaked.

"How did you get away so fast, I followed you out the door?" he asked.

"Like I said, if you had time to care, you would know!" I fired back.

"I'm asking you now Zen!"

I didn't know what to do, what did I have to lose? I was angry, perhaps my rage would help me explain more succinctly.

"I died Ash. What did you think had happened to me when I went missing all those years ago? I adored you. I wouldn't have just run away. I died, I rose to another place,

I was made into an angel, assigned to help dying people but I fell, I fell and I got bitten, bitten by yet another being I hadn't known existed, and I became one, except my blood is all mixed up now, so I don't belong anywhere. I thought I could save you Ash, but what is the point of saving someone who can't stand you?"

His expression wasn't one of surprise; it almost read 'Fair enough'. It changed as my tears fell for the first time in his presence. He walked up to me and held me really tight as I cried in his arms.

"THERE SHE IS!" I heard a group of deep aggressive voices shout.

"Zen?" Ash questioned, holding my arms tight and looking down to gage my reaction.

I froze. The commotion with Ash had made me forget I was running from otherworldly beings, soldiers of some sort of evil who were trying to exterminate me.

I had underestimated Ash, "Bite me!" he said.

"What?" I asked.

He held me tighter and his lips met mine, briefly but sincerely, "Bite me. Turn me Zen," he repeated.

Perhaps the rain was meant to be. The wet cobbles and raindrops in their eyes held them up as they tried to run towards me. I had seconds to make the right decision. If I didn't turn Ash now then I may never have the opportunity again. I lowered my teeth to his neck ready, he let go of his hold on my arms and clenched his fists anticipating the pain he might feel. I hesitated, now wasn't the time to change him. I pushed him over to the wall of Exeter College, he couldn't move his leg; it was not broken just hurt, as I planned. I leapt to the opposite high wall, gripping on to the top tightly with my right hand whilst reaching with my left for one of the hidden swords I kept in the city, this one in the cross support of the wall. My executioners were seconds from my delicate human Ash.

"You even think about laying a claw on him and I'll make sure you suffer the most horrific deaths imaginable," I shouted as their sights moved to me.

Gracefully I glided from the high wall kicking one of the three demons. They drew their weapons but didn't foresee my advantage of being a left-handed swordswoman. Off went the first of their heads with my first swipe. The one I had kicked was nearly on my back, niftily I plunged the sword under my arm behind me into his heart dodging his swing. The third was circling me as I turned to him. He reached for an arrow on his back but too slow for my reaction found himself with my sword in his foot; perfect aim. I lifted him up by the collar with my right grip and retrieved my blade. Releasing my anger I plunged him at the wall where I heard his skull shatter. It was gruesome but purely out of self-defence. I hesitated before looking at Ash. He couldn't run with a hurt leg but I expected neither would he want to see me again. There weren't any words. All I could do was glance at him shamefully. I didn't enjoy taking lives but I had had enough of mine being taken, and besides these were demons, not innocent lives that I was taking. He didn't seem too startled; perhaps he hadn't really taken any of it in yet.

"I'll help you back to your old place and you won't see me again," I said with my head down.

"If I hadn't wanted to see you again I wouldn't have come for you tonight" he replied.

I smiled, unbelievingly. "We must go back to mine and retrieve anything we want to take but then we'll have to move on, it's not safe."

"Where do you propose we go?" he enquired.

"The castle, I know a tunnel to get into the crypt, there are lots of ways in that haven't been discovered, that's the safest place at the moment."

"The castle?" he countered.

"You scared?"

"No, just, not the most..." he searched for words.

"No, it's not, but it's the safest."

"Zen, earlier, you, I thought you were going to..." Again he couldn't think how to complete his sentence.

"We'll talk about it later Ash, now we need to go."

I gave him a hand up, the touch of his hand weakened me but I had to be strong to get us to safety and then work out if this life really was for him.

The castle was our safe haven for tonight, he was cold; the best I could offer him was one of the blankets from the exhibition in the prison complex but we had to stay in the crypt. He'd topped up the poison in his system and drifted away temporarily. I wondered if he would dream or just be out of it for a time. I pressed play on my iPod, Bowie was my blanket in this ridiculous existence. I couldn't let my guard down after the attack earlier tonight but I could reminisce in my mind...

* * *

July 2005

He really hurt me at times. Mainly when he was with junkies, trying to show off to earn a share of the hit they were off to score. The drug had complete control of him. When he was withdrawing he'd be sweet to anyone in exchange of a promise to earn half of a dig to get his strength and disguise the pain from its infection for a few hours. Whoever held the cash held the key to the heroin; anyone else was in the way, an obstacle to be pushed aside. I wanted to be forgiving, to believe that he was sorry about how he'd acted. I kept telling myself he would be, that he would rely on the drug only until he had the strength to work towards escaping from it, but if that was true it would only have been smack he craved. I kept my hopes to myself, for the moment the drugs were convenient as I could find him when I wanted his company. I was also scared that he wouldn't want to know me if he could better his life. I tried to time it so he would be stoned when I saw him, so that he wouldn't rather be making a raise. I swore I saw his true colours when he was in this state, the charming, caring guy who was being hopelessly consumed by the drug. I walked a few circuits of the city, avoiding where he made his raise. If he was stoned he'd be somewhere other than there. I caught sight of him on George Street.

Hopefully I'd 'casually' walk into him and we'd go somewhere and hang with a few beers. Or rather he'd drink and smoke, I'd admire him soberly. I had to believe that the guy I was falling for was the real him, the cruel side of him I sometimes saw had to be the craving. We talked about so much; he understood everything, made me feel better about anything or anyone who was trying to knock me down. He was my living guardian. I was sure of it. My biggest fear was the drug taking him away from me.

* * *

As I woke from my reminiscence I felt confused. The distant memory worried me. I'd seen the harsher side of him more recently, like the drugs had swallowed his personality and his obsession with them was ninety per cent of him. I still loved him. He never loved me, he couldn't. I wasn't stunning and picture perfect as he was. I would have been satisfied with being loved like family or a friend but was I just a cash pot? It hurt like nothing in the world. Death had hurt less. Would I be able to rescue him if he was like me, or would I lose him if he was free of drugs? I had to pretend that I was worth more to give me the courage to at least give him a chance at a better life. He had asked me to. Then maybe he did care and I was just being blind and paranoid. I decided there was no choice, when he woke I would have to gamble.

For the first time in a long time I had managed to sleep and so when I began to come too again it took me a few minutes to properly awaken, like coming out of one of those vivid dreams where you question who and where you are. I remembered feeling the stone against my head. It was then I remembered where we were. I looked up to the corner in which Ash had drifted off to sleep. It was then the alarm rang through me as I couldn't hear his pulse. I glided up with an unconscious leap. As I surfaced I pulled the makeshift blanket from him and felt his skin. It was nearly as cold as mine. I could hear his pulse now but it was so faint, so quiet. His last dose of 'medication' was to be his final one. Despite being cold, his spiked hair and marble white face was soaked with sweat. His eyelids were black and lips blue. I had hardly any time to save him. I exposed my teeth but my attempted resuscitation was interrupted. I heard a crash as the crypt door was broken, footsteps, very light footsteps followed until a blinding light manifested.

"Emma?" I addressed the angel who stood behind us, in surprise.

"Zen, you've got to let him go," she said.

"And what of me, Emma?" I questioned.

"You've interfered with the grand scheme of things enough. I'm sorry for your fate but did you not learn anything from falling Zena?"

"Yes, I learnt I would do anything for this man."

"You were banished from our realm for tormenting him, for not accompanying those who needed a guide to the next world."

"I was his guardian, I did not ask to die, not to be given a duty, I simply used my duty to protect him."

"And you still can't leave him alone. Let him go Zena. The Higher Powers have been talking, you already have hell dimensions on your back for being different, for spreading truth of their existence to humans, you don't want two enemies, do you?" She spoke reasonably but not compassionately.

"Let me just say good bye," I pleaded.

She nodded. And then I remembered what Silas had once told me. Emma was in fact giving me a window to save Ash but against the wishes of the Higher Powers. I had to play along to avoid her getting into trouble.

I'd wasted a couple of minutes; already his pulse had faded to a whisper.

I mistook his voice for it. "Zen."

I looked into his eyes to see him looking back. "Turn me," he said again. He had come round from the touch of my hand.

I let my eyes close slowly but heavily, I lowered my head to his heart, the pulse was strongest there, with Emma's eyes sharp on me I kissed his chest. In a blink of her eyes I sunk my teeth into his heart and drank as fast as I could. His blood was electric; I felt the power of his life running through my veins, once I had felt butterflies inside me being near him, now angels were swirling around my chest with the racing beat of my heart which had temporarily restarted. I could feel Emma trying to pull me away but I was too insentient to the world, only him and I existed. I embraced him tightly with one arm whilst I reached for the small dagger down my sock. Again I could feel her hand battling mine as I pulled it from its sheath. My strength had just multiplied and I effortlessly drew the dagger to my chest, ripping my shirt, I sliced an 'x' over my heart. His eyes were closed now, I had weakened him completely. He only had to take a little of my blood; the cut was deep enough, blood flooded to his lips as they met my breast. The darkness around his eyes faded and he became pure again, he was radiant, his hair blacker than before, the pattern in his eyes became sharper and his skin took on a translucent quality; a beautiful angelic vampire. The world came crashing back like a hangover following a night where the room had been spinning.

"May the Powers have mercy on you both," Emma said turning her back on us, the crypt too narrow to fly she faded making herself unseen as she left us. But before she had completely disappeared I caught a brief smile and wink, a secret congratulation. From where she came from we were failures but I had faith, I knew we would change the world and I knew not everyone shunned us. It may have felt like an eternity but I had won the life of the guy I loved. Oxford was our city now. I couldn't wait to start getting to know this crazy vampiric angel Ash, the purest version of him, no drugs, no death awaiting us, no secrets.

25th December 2013

"We'll always be as young as we are now Zen, we have eternity, it's crazy, there's so much to explore!" Ash said proudly, holding my hand as we sat together, our legs dangling over the Bridge of Sighs. The snow sprinkled around us, its carpet of white settling thick on the cobbles and road below us. I admired the blood dyed snow heart Ash had surprised me with. I put my head against his shoulder, his arm around me. I finally had my perfect ending, happiness, my best friend, my guardian angel.

Astral Walker

21st September 2014

'Punk' everyone called him because he was popular and good looking; no one knew his true name or his secret. He studied at the university as a post grad. He spent a lot of time in his books, but he liked to party too. He didn't have time for relationships and he didn't keep friends as such, more a following. It was wearing being popular. He resided in his own top floor flat of a shared house on Abingdon Road, away from the other residents. This September afternoon the rain was pouring down heavily. Punk peered at the blurry window; it was hard to see much out of it, just a smeared view of the tennis courts across the road. He had a funny feeling he was being watched. That should be impossible with the many locks he had bolted on the door. He tried to shake off the feeling. Placing his book flat on his writing bureau he adjusted his position, elbow on the desk, and head in hand. No, it was worse now, like someone on a bus looking over shoulder. He knew the place was haunted but this was too intense. He swiftly turned around. Both of them jumped, Punk fell sideways out of his chair, landing harshly on the floor against the drawers, his hand clutching up on the green leather lining of the desk. She had jumped back too in shock.

"Am I dreaming?" she asked.

"How did you get in?" Punk quickly looked towards the door confused; it was still as bolted as it had been when he had secured it.

"Am I dead?" she returned another question.

Her confusion overrode his initial fear. He stood up, slowly walking to her; looking to her eyes reassuringly he reached for her hand. He half expected his to fall straight through it, assuming she was the first vivid spirit he would see. Shivers scuttled down his back as the touch of her physical self was apparent. She was real, human, or so he presumed. There was no way she could have gotten in.

"You're not dead," he concluded, "or dreaming."

"I, I, remember being in hospital, I think I was involved in an attack," she recalled.

"Great, well, I will call the John Radcliffe; see if you are under their care." Punk reached for his mobile, found the number for the local hospital and tapped 'call'. He put his arm out towards the desk chair, gesturing for her to sit.

"Can you remember your name?" he asked, as the phone rang. Neglecting the detail of how she'd got into his flat, he wondered if she had somehow wandered from the hospital undetected.

"Louisa Ebbes," she replied softly. She sat very still, in shock, trying to make some sense of how she had manifested randomly in this unsuspecting stranger's residence.

Punk had walked into the next room. "Ok, thank you, and you're sure? Ok." He hung up the phone. Looking rather pale he spoke, "So, yes you were taken to the JR, and you're still there, very much alive, but in a coma,"

"Ok," she said.

"Hang on, I've read about this, I'm sure. A friend, she, well it sounds a little weird but she kind of does this thing for a job. I research some stuff for her from time to time, let me check my books." Punk reached to the large book collection left of the desk. "Ok, here we go, 'Only one known account has ever been recorded of astral walkers, where in a coma the subject is able to manifest in human form in search of answers to their recent misfortune. It is believed to happen in attempted vampire transformation.'"

"Come again?" Louisa questioned.

"Do you remember being bitten and ... never mind." Punk, noticed the puncture wounds hiding behind her long blonde hair. "I think you may have been the victim of a vampire attack, though looks like they didn't quite manage to turn you, they must have been disturbed. We need to find the attacker."

She looked at Punk as if he was crazy.

To which he returned; "How else can you explain the wounds, and randomly turning up in my room? Let's take a walk, you can stay at my place, I'll get advice from my friend in the morning. I guess this is surreal, maybe just believe you are dreaming, except be careful, I assume any damage done will be permanent."

She quite liked him; he was kind and exceptionally accommodating.

She took his hand which he held out.

* * *

It was hard to ignore the rhythmic beeping of the hospital machinery. She was present in three places, a corporeal body lying on life support in a hospital bed of the John Radcliffe; also as a spectral astral version wandering some poor guy's abode and finally in this weird dream, this dream that didn't seem to require much thought, just presence.

Wherever she was it was black, black like death, darker than darkness itself. Some alternative slow tone music played faintly in the background, a female voice wove through it like waves of the sea until a male's lead vocal spoke in song, an angel perhaps? Did she have to fight through the segmented existences she had been split into or just endure them?

As far as she could tell she was sitting. A flicker of candle light out of the corner of her eye startled her; naturally she couldn't resist turning her head in its direction. She caught sight of a man; it was hard to put an exact age on him in just flickering yellow light, late thirties perhaps.

"I thought you could use some light," he said.

"Thanks," she replied, a shadow of a thought scurried through her mind but it was too fast to grasp hold of.

"I think it gets better with time."

"It does," she said, getting more used to this fluid form of communication.

"The thoughts – at the moment you're not in control of them, of the dream, you're almost like a puppet, unable to realise what it is you need to say, or consciously be aware of anything too much. I think I've been here some time. The sound of the heart monitor beeping has become almost natural to my ears, and then this music faded in just now; I had a feeling that I wasn't alone."

"So how did you get the candle?" she said without having to consciously think the thought.

"Ah, see you're getting the hang of it now – managing to say things, though I expect you weren't aware you were going to say that before I heard it. The candle was kind of the same, it sort of appeared and I then realised I had wanted it," he informed her.

She stared into the darkness, lifeless, thoughtless. She wanted to speak but as each thought merged it slipped.

A few minutes passed.

"Nasty bite you have there," he said.

Then just like that she was curious. "Why are you here?"

"Overdose, I'm in a coma I think, just like you."

"Overdose?"

"Street drugs."

"Oh, ok, so not the hospital's screw up?"

"Not yet," he smiled.

She laughed; she made herself jump at the sound of her own laughter.

"Hey how did you know they were bites?"

"Because I read a lot – gothic horror plus spending time around the streets it's not really hard to believe that such things could happen."

"You're not the first person to tell me that you know?"

"Yeah?"

"It's weird but I think I'm not just here. I have some recollection of another guy, quite muscular, long spiked multi coloured hair, eighties punk sort of look, he claimed the same. And last thing I can remember was sitting in his flat."

"It's not impossible – there are all sorts of myths and legends to do with vampires and Oxford has a long line of secret history to back it up."

She was starting to snatch her thoughts a little easier as they whizzed through her mind now but still not as fluent as in awakening.

"So, where are we?" she asked.

"I think we have somehow channelled into each other's minds whilst we lay in unconsciousness, in terms of where we are in the dream – I don't know."

"Well, I don't see why we can't go somewhere else. Fancy trying?" she asked; her mind easing as the fluency of thought seemed to slowly, gradually be returning.

No sooner had she put forward the suggestion a gentle ice cold breeze surrounded her from both sides, particularly around her hands and neck which were not covered by the hospital garment. The air rested on her skin reminding herself of the presence of her limbs. She could feel her fingers curled around the sides of the hospital bed.

The guy who had been illuminated by candle light was now standing next to her bedside.

"Take my hand," he said.

She did and as she did she was even more aware of her ability to move. She supported her blood drained body with her free hand on the metal bed guard and jumped lightly to the floor which she realised she was grateful to feel. If this was a regular dream the likelihood was she would currently be free falling into nothingness.

"Hey you did it!" he said releasing his grip on her hand.

"I did!" she exclaimed. She instinctively put her arms out and held his drug devoured body close. He was taller than her, and so she rested her head against his chest. With his candle free arm he embraced her. They did not seem to know one another but they would both have to rely on the other to get through this strange journey.

The bitterness of the previously gentle breeze was now no longer in wisps, it had become the room. Their own breaths were visible before them, though only just, despite the intensity of the cold the very lives in them were threatening to fade. They parted their embrace to address the reason for the frost, it was then they noticed a door amidst the darkness had appeared.

"Shall we go forward?" she dared him.

He did not speak, but gestured in agreement.

"First, tell me your name," she demanded.

She didn't know what fate awaited them beyond the door and wanted to at least know the name of this guy.

"'Blake'," she thought he said.

"I'm Louisa," she returned.

"You ready Louisa?"

"Not sure." The chaos of the music that still permeated the atmosphere was drowning out any of her attempts at lateral thinking.

She felt Blake's hand once again as he prompted her forward and reached for the round brass door handle, the candle had seemingly disappeared. "Close your eyes, keep them closed until I say, Ok?"

She did as he asked, holding tightly to his shaky hand and trusting him to lead her forward blindly.

She had a feeling they were through the door, the deep thought proofing music had gone and the bitter air felt a little freer. She felt un-paralysed, able to move and think as she would in waking life. A lot of chatter seemed to be surrounding them, she could still feel Blake's hand, and they had stopped.

"Listen Louisa, when you open your eyes I want you to look at me, nothing else, just look at me for a minute."

She gently released her eyes looking straight up into Blake's, the bluish grey tone of light in this space almost blinded her.

"I've had this dream before, we are surrounded by millions of people; they are heading for a ferry, a ferry to the afterlife. It's easy to be tempted to follow, a sensation of peace will tempt you; you could lose your focus just like in the room we were in before, fog will try and creep into your mind, don't let it. We need to talk to each other, find another door," Blake explained holding her forearms to keep her focus.

"I understand," she said.

They began to walk over a metallic floor, in the opposite direction to all the souls drifting to board a large ferry.

"Blake, you seem to know your way about, have you been here before?"

"Yes, but not in hospital. I was resuscitated by a mate last time but had a long recovery sleeping, I only remember this. I saw people I knew going for the boat, I later found out they had died."

"Is that why it is so cold here?"

"No, it's not cold here; our bodies are cold, slipping away from reality. I believe it's up to you to make a decision, are you ready to die, do you want to return to living or are you undecided?"

"What if I'm undecided?"

"You wander, wander the depths of your own mind, all the millions of miles tidied away in unconsciousness are unfolded here for you to explore, except it looks like we're in this together, so..."

"What if we awaken from our comas, do we remember this?"

"Little bits, it will just feel like a strange dream."

"But will I remember you?" she asked. He turned his head and looked down to her as they walked. His eyes staring into hers, the start of the first silent connection they would encounter. It was an exchange of deep thoughts that communicated their mutual feelings for one another.

"I don't know," he replied with a strain in his voice trying to disguise the swelling of his throat, and impact of the blow to his chest at the realisation of possibly losing her. It was as if his own memory had refreshed itself and he knew of her.

"Then I'll stay undecided for a little while," she replied.

They walked for a while enduring the live connection they seemed to have sparked with the touch of one another's hands. They were at peace, and would occasionally look at the other in unison with a mirrored expression of bliss. They could have easily been tempted to turn back to the ferry but the current of emotions chasing through their veins was keeping their focus.

'I think I've found my soul mate,' she considered silently.

'This girl, it's like she is a part of me,' he thought.

'It's like we're...' "...connected." They spoke harmoniously, followed by a nervous laugh.

"How can it be that I feel happier, more settled in this non-material world; more so than I've ever felt in waking life?" Louisa asked Blake, expecting him to have the answer.

"Because you know that nothing bad can actually happen to you here, have you ever felt pain in a dream?"

She thought for a moment. "What about pleasure?"

"And I'd ask you the same question again, but hope that this time the answer is yes." Blake smiled a cocky smile.

They'd reached a group of buildings which looked bomb struck, the roofs were caved in and the outer paintwork flaking, not particularly inviting. In just a blink as Louisa's glance returned, Blake looked different, wearing a sharp suit and trilby hat which he flipped from his head into his hand gesturing her to enter into a now classy coffee shop. As she blinked again he was back in his hospital gown. She invited Blake to go ahead taking the open door from him. She wasn't self-conscious about looking him up and down as she followed.

* * *

"Louisa?" a voice said; it was familiar and not only was the voice familiar but so was the warmth she felt around her.

Involuntarily her eyes fluttered; as they did a window of blurred colours grasped her attention away from the darkness. Slowly she decided to wake, instantly she recognised Punk, though in the flat the lighting seemed a lot brighter than she remembered before.

"You were out for a while; here I made you a sweet tea." Punk handed her the hot beverage in hope of keeping her conscious. "Maybe we should give that walk a miss tonight, eh? I think you passed out, I didn't realise that would be possible in your, er, condition."

"No, nor did I. Thanks, for the drink. I had this dream that I met this guy and we were trying to walk away from life and death, just running away in our own paradise. You know I think he may have been the devil. How ridiculous is that," Louisa explained, a little disorientated.

Punk looked both alarmed and deeply concerned.

"That may not have been a dream Louisa. I did some research whilst you were out and this business is really complicated. When I read the passage earlier I was stupid not to turn the page. You are stuck between life and death because you must be half way through a siring. The vampire who bit you aimed to turn you but you couldn't have consumed enough of their blood to start the process. The only way to reverse the process is to kill the vampire with a blade laced in your blood. I think I found your incident's report in the Mail and if I'm right, you were found in Albion Place. If that is the case River, my slayer friend, patrolled and dusted a record number of vamps that same evening in that location. If she dusted your sire then I'm afraid you are stuck in this state until you decide to die. However, the journalist report also mentioned a second casualty that night. If I'm not mistaken the guy in your dream is probably the vampire that attempted to sire you. Because of the circumstances; I mean because he was dusted amidst a siring, it is possible his body would have returned to the human he was before he was sired himself. So that leads me to believe his life could be sacrificed for your own. But it would mean taking an innocent human life for another. I'm afraid the information available to me is unverified and could be misleading as there is very little really known on the subject."

Without really taking in everything Punk had said Louisa could only think of Blake. "And if that was the case the vampire could have died that night as a human?"

"I guess – if fate decided it was to be. Why? No don't answer that – I'm with you, you think your destinies are entwined. You're both in a coma as humans, you're thinking of the second victim I mentioned, the victim who previously may have been your sire."

"If this is so, will our circumstances be parallel? Will we either both live, both die, both be indefinitely in this spirit world?"

"I can't give you that answer now Louisa but give me some time to find out." Punk said. "May I ask; does your question concern the wellbeing of your freedom or your unity with this other being?"

"Punk, let me return your question with one of my own. If you had been torn through the impossible, waking knowingly as an astral walker whilst your body lay in the lurch, and then walked through another awakening with someone who seems to have some sort of blissful power over you, would you want to return to this material world alone?"

"I'll find your answer Louisa," Punk said understandingly. "It's late, unless anything unforeseen happens tomorrow then I will be completely committed to helping you through this hell, no matter what path you choose."

Little did Punk know that he would be called to assist the slayer in a city crisis come ten-fifteen tomorrow morning but in the mean time Louisa would be decrypting her mind through her dream world reality, unknowing of whatever crisis the world was facing.

* * *

The coffee shop was quite dark, in some ways it looked more like a cocktail bar than a cafe.

"I'm going to grab us a table, an Americano for me," Blake said.

'An Ameri- what? Obviously Blake was used to these classy coffee bars.' Louisa panicked mentally.

"A what sorry?" she asked in the hope she'd just misheard terribly.

"An Americano," Blake repeated.

No, that just made the situation a whole lot worse as the horror and confusion was apparent in her expression on realising she in fact hadn't misheard just was completely unfamiliar of the term. It was ok, she could just look at the menu and try and recognise what the hell he wanted. Oh, they didn't have regular coffee? What kind of dream was this? Well she would just have to have an Americano with him. Bravely she struggled to take the drinks to the table without spilling them and then on tasting to her surprise and a little mortification she realised Americano was in fact just normal coffee. Blake smiled witnessing Louisa's inability to cope with a fairly easy social situation. Louisa realised that each door they passed through was an opportunity to grasp a little bit more control of humanity. Even if awkward the coffee confusion was amusing and a step closer to Blake, she was really looking forward to the conversation to follow.

He sat back sinking into the low leather chair completely at ease. It hugged him, devoured him and even in its arms he still looked in control.

"Something's on your mind," he said.

Louisa was taken by surprise at his concern, not that she thought him incapable of it but maybe too vain to voice it.

"I guess I thought I was in two places at once or three if you include my body. I believed I existed in those places all at once, in parallel time, but when we entered the coffee shop I think I woke up in that guy's flat. He said some stuff."

Not even a micro expression could be detected in Blake's face, he was composed, ready to hear what Louisa was about to reveal.

She continued, "He said that it might be impossible to wake from this coma, the siring process was interrupted and so the vampire returned to himself, how he would have been as a human - before eternal life. Something that is bothering me however; what if when he was sired he was already dying, perhaps from an overdose. And that would be an uncanny link to you and I don't you agree?"

"Have you then asked yourself what interest a vampire would have in siring you, not just drinking you? What was your life before this accident? Had you wanted this eternal life?"

"I cannot recall anything of my life, though I have to admit even if my thoughts were suppressed on awakening in this reality, something deep within me which required no thought told me to trust you."

"There are in fact so many possibilities then are there not? Of you and me, but something deep within you allowed faith in me, it would be fortunate if I had my memories of my life."

"Of course, and you do have memories of your life before this coma, you've spoken of how you've been here before and how you died." With an acceptable amount of urgency Louisa pleaded to hear the piece of this missing puzzle. She also wondered why she had been surprised at Blake's concern, she had only known him unconsciously for a little while and in that time there was nothing to base a comparison on. The more she reassessed her own reactions she realised there must have been something between them so much deeper. She could feel his eyes on her but not as a threat, instead a silent comfort calmly supporting her as the coffee shop allowed her mind to wander into the depths of the past...

* * *

The atmosphere felt urgent, even awkward. The surrounding buildings were grey, a metaphor of the life they absorbed. She felt out of place, uneasy in this rough part of the city, especially this late. She caught sight of him walking toward her and she felt a little safer. No-one ever gave him trouble; he kept himself to himself and somehow had the respect of everyone else.

"Hey, so you still up for hanging out, I was worried, hadn't heard from you for a while." Her flaw was being unable to hide her need for him. She would spend all the hours in a day evaluating her successes and failures in their friendship. She knew that had she been able to live a little more carelessly, then things between them may not have been so screwed up. She couldn't trust fate enough not to feel the need to grasp on to hope continuously. Just lately she had grown up a little and this enabled her to take a few deep breaths and let go, seeing him again she felt all the better for it.

"You don't need to worry. Let's go shall we?" He said casually, perhaps with some locked away thoughts behind his words which Louisa realised he wouldn't be sharing. She only really wanted to hear those words if they were to be of comfort. She'd rather live in a constant state of uncertainty about whether she would be rejected by him than to actually endure it.

"So, how've you been?" he asked.

She searched for the best answer, "Yeah, good thanks, you?"

He stopped; there was a look of hesitation in his expression, something she hadn't seen before. "Sweetheart, I'm sorry we haven't spent a lot of time together recently, I know you want it to be like old times, I've just been busy with things, but something's happened and, well, it turns out I could make up for it."

Her heart stopped, or at least she thought it had but then the numbness passed and the thumping against her chest reminded her she hadn't replied.

Was this too good to be true, did she really want this decade of a desire to be realised or just to continue to live in the drama of anticipating it.

She removed her gaze from the pavement and to his eyes, his beautiful eyes.

He didn't say anything more, just guided her to a quieter area, away from the eyes of the city's incoming traffic.

She couldn't quite believe he was kissing her. Then there was the searing pain, his teeth sunk into her neck but she didn't resist, she embraced it.

* * *

His eyes were still on her as her focus returned to him in the coffee shop.

"Blake?" she questioned as if she had only just set eyes on him since the incident in Albion Place.

"So, it's not quite how I had thought it would turn out but didn't I say we'd hang out a little more?"

Everything had changed in the moment of realisation; she had unconsciously built up a carefree bond with Blake in this dream just as she'd wished she could have done in the past but now she was facing him, the guy whose presence she used to be intimidated by.

"So where do we go from here?" she asked.

"Where do you want to go love?" he returned; his voice familiar now, the soft decisive tone which sent enchantment through her.

Stopping her from returning to the awkward juvenile that was threatening to revisit she considered the flash back she had just replayed. Somehow his new vampire self had wanted her but had he always wanted her, would it be too brash to suggest a new life together.

"What do you say to escaping the drag of life and starting again on our own together? We must be the first to do this, to resist the ferry, so who's to say we can't rule this place? Together with our minds in tune we can have anything we want, live for free and however we want – it's purely imagination right?" Louisa proposed.

Blake stood up; his hospital rags were fading away and transforming into a dapper suit, the trilby that had earlier flashed before Louisa's eyes was now sat in the chair which Blake had retired from not far from a long black coat neatly resting over the arm.

He walked over to Louisa who had followed his lead and also stood. He put his hand on her shoulder and bowed his head to whisper in her ear, "Shall we find out what is through the next door?"

She fluttered her eyelids with a discreet smile, she took his arm which he held out for her leaving a stride of innocence behind at each step she took with him to the far end of the coffee shop.

* * *

"You're with us again then?" Punk said.

"I've made a decision Punk; I accept it is probably impossible to wake up corporeally in the reality I once knew, in this world you walk, in which my body lies. I want to remain in the astral plane this other me walks with the man who indeed began to sire me as I recall I desired." Louisa said almost robotically.

"Well, she's sure of herself," a voice which Louisa didn't recognise, spoke.

"Louisa, please meet my friend, River, the slayer of Oxford."

"Hey girl you've missed a whole near apocalypse,

zombie trouble!" River blurted out, probably in an outburst of relief.

Louisa shook her head a little in dismissal of the details for what she just heard. "I'll leave that at 'near apocalypse'."

"Wise kid," a further voice called from another room.

"And, urgh, meet Ash and Zen, vamps, but nice vamps." Punk threw in quickly in hope that Louisa didn't quite hear and ask for the longer explanation.

"Look I don't want to be any more imposing than I have been already, I can see you've been busy and have been kind enough to do some research for me as well. I want to ask you one last favour that perhaps is impossible but given the impossibility of your guests it may not be so weird."

"Shoot," said the female vamp who Louisa had thought was introduced as Zen.

"Let me just get to the point, Blake and I want to run the astral plane in which our bodies walk, would a little magick and a vampire bite be too much to ask?" Louisa asked weakly in some doubt.

"You're already dead honey, how's a vamp bite going to work?" River said not keen on producing more vamps.

"No, she's not quite dead and besides her astral form which we see before us is somehow corporeal, it wouldn't be impossible," Punk suggested.

"It's worth a shot, and Riv' it's not like she's going to be a bad-ass, she'll have been bitten by one of us, vampiric angels, their nature would be one with ours," Ash added.

"And why the magick?" River interrogated.

"To transform the retched drab death port to something else, giving spirits the chance to wander whilst they come to terms with their mortal choice, instead of so many disturbed ghosts on earth they would be with us. We would be an ally, any day you would need our support we would have an army and another realm to offer." Louisa made her argument strongly and convincingly.

Punk, Ash and Zen waited for the approval of River. "Lucky for you I've just come into contact with a very powerful witch with a special connection to the Gods, it will take more than a little magick but I can't see why it shouldn't be possible." River smiled, losing the bitter front she had displayed before now.

"Thank you, I hope one day we can repay your kindness," Louisa said genuinely.

"I'm sure the opportunity will present itself," River replied.

"And thank you Punk, the Gods were smiling on me when they delivered me to your abode."

"The Gods always smile on their soldiers," Punk returned. "Take care now, won't you Louisa."

"So, who's to do the honours?" River asked Ash and Zen.

"Both of them," Punk commanded, "To be sure it will work and that the venom will be strong enough to reach Louisa's lover in the other world. Just make sure you exchange blood with him as soon as you return."

Ash and Zen looked at each other smiling at the thought of fresh voluntary human blood. Before Louisa could change her mind the excruciating pain from two pairs of fangs allowed her to scream as she gave up her life. She felt their blood trickle into her throat making her one of them. Her body faded from Punk's apartment. The heart monitor in the hospital drew a straight line.

* * *

Louisa had no idea how long had passed in the real world where she had now let her body give up and had taken Blake's with her. However long it had been, it was obviously enough time for the slayer to have got in touch with her witch, as Louisa and Blake now lived in Oxford's castle in this new between life reality. Oxford's spirits wandered the astral plane of the city as they pleased, taking time to decide their fate. Blake joined Louisa at the top of St George's tower and looked over their creation.

"I knew you could do what I'd tried to start, an eternal life together. How much better you managed it. Not just eternal life, but a castle to live in and a world to guide the spirits of Oxford in," he said. "And the warm chamber awaiting us isn't bad either."

"You're right, I did do a good job, for here you stand before me not only irresistible, but wanting me."

Blake embraced Louisa and whispered to her once again as he guided her back inside, "I always wanted you."

Death from Dreaming Spires

It was a Monday morning of September 2014. Ten fifteen to be exact. A few people scurried through the city centre running late for a ten o'clock start for work, others were casual shoppers. Summer was over and the bulk of the tourists had gone home. The city centre was nearly silent; a little shock still filled the atmosphere with the news of yesterday's jumper from St Mary the Virgin church's tower. As pedestrians made their way up the High Street some noticed the bloody trail of footprints on the pavement. There were a couple of police officers scattered about. Naturally most people thought the blood was a temporary time capsule of an incident of the weekend. A little way up the road there was no noise, no screaming, and no warning. It happened so suddenly that it was fortunate not a single passerby was hit. The rough sleeper hurtled to the pavement, twisted and broken. His mouth covered in blood, no one realised the blood had not belonged to him and was on his face before he jumped. No-one could move, frozen in shock. It would remain a mystery, for now, why he had jumped from Carfax Tower. There were speculations and assumptions. He was a familiar rough sleeper, perhaps he had wanted to end his life. As far as anyone knew no-one had pushed him, or had they? People gossiped in the crowd.

Perhaps he had not been pushed physically, but the bite that marked the start of his mutation into a zombie was also the push for him to take his own life. People had once called him selfish, scum, filth, although had he been true to those labels he would not have jumped from the tower in order to prevent himself from infecting others with a bite from his already flesh hungry lips.

A girl smiled a wickedly satisfied smile and walked on whilst others began to exchange looks, negotiating who would call an ambulance. It was too late for the hero; he had accomplished what he had wanted.

"Can everyone stand back please; an ambulance is on its way," an American police officer ordered. He radioed in, "Yes, this is Steve; we have another jumper, Carfax, IC1, I need 11-41, severely injured, though possibly DOE."

"What do we have here?" a taller, paler, white haired, British officer asked his colleague, "Looks like a junkie."

"Have some respect man keep your voice down, this is the second in a week. I expect the squad will be looking into this?" Steve didn't like the way the senior PC referred to the victim, addict or not the circumstances were tragic.

River had been overwhelmed lately with new comer vamps, Ash and Zen, living it large. She had made a deal; they could stay if they only preyed on humans who would be a nuisance to the city, murderers and what have you; it would keep the crime rate down. And besides they were part angels, seemed harsh to dust them when they could be an asset. Then there was Punk's strange new girl friend, wandering around alive whilst her body was in a coma. If that wasn't enough a witch called Bow had tracked her down looking for assistance on some guy she was destined to protect. River knew all about destiny, her destiny was to be one of the many slayers. Her jurisdiction was the city of Oxford and everything evil that tried to claim the lives of its people were her targets. River knew today that this was not a straight forward suicide but she couldn't get close enough to make her own conclusions. She would have to ask Damien, the city's coroner. If anything curious came back at the inquest he would let her know. It had taken her a while to build up an army of contacts but without them her job would be a lot harder. There was not much she could do for now. It seemed an inconvenience to walk around the city centre when she would normally climb the tower, using the rooftops to take her where she needed to be, but she couldn't take the risk of being seen in circumstances like these. She blended in pulling out her mobile from her black zip hoody and strode off in her purple Thai fisherman's trousers.

'D, take urgent interest in Carfax jumper. Let me know if anything suspicious. Riv,' she tapped into her phone, and sent the text to the coroner.

Like everyone else, all she could do was wait, though it wasn't long before more evidence surfaced.

Screams emerged from the Covered Market. River ran towards the High Street, people were flooding out of the market's entrances, like rats from a sewer. Defaced, blood wrenched creatures followed with handfuls of meat, obviously taken from the butchers. They didn't seem satisfied with the freshness as they shuffled as fast as they could after the human livestock. River took a knife from her belt then threw it at one of the creatures. It hit the heart. The creature groaned, and with all its strength heaved the blade from its chest.

"I never miss," River said aloud.

"You didn't miss." A voice said. River looked behind her shoulder to the shadow by the Edinburgh Woollen Mill. It was Ash.

Zen stood next to him, "They're indestructible."

"I noticed," River moaned. "Sorry, can I borrow this?" She took a bike from a cyclist trying to make an escape. Ripping the wheel from the frame, she then peeled off the tyre. The metal framework was soon ripping through the air; it took off the head of one of the creatures. "Not indestructible, just a zombie, watch the movies! Decapitation seems to work well."

"Good observation, but how do we decapitate all of them?" Zen offered.

"Lampost?" Ash suggested.

The three of them looked at one another.

"You guide these people to safety, avoid snacking, and I'll take care of these," River ordered.

"How are you going to take them all out?" Zen questioned.

"I'm not; I'm going to lock them in there!" River gestured at the gates of the Covered Market.

Zen and Ash held up a huge umbrella, luckily it was a cloudy day but still, the less daylight exposure the better. They went on with the crowds trying to safely accommodate them.

"Marks and Spencer?" Zen suggested.

"Spencer's," Ash agreed.

River ripped up the traffic signal and raced at the fleet of zombies, determined to destroy as many as she could and imprison the rest.

It was worth a shot anyway.

In went River's ear plugs, she selected The Script's albums on her mp3 player. The upbeat, feel good rhythm seemed fitting for this job. She swore if she died on a job it would be Bowie circulating her brain, but she wasn't going to die today. The first flock of zombies were decapitated and scattered over the High Street. Buses had been abandoned; the police weren't quite sure what to do. River had ordered them to take care of the public. She trusted Zen and Ash but hadn't had time to do a head count in case the odd person had became too tempting for their blood thirst. If the fuzz were around they would probably be more likely to behave themselves, probably. River hadn't been too keen on the taller, plumper, white haired, officer who confronted her, the same one who had been unprofessional talking to his colleague earlier. Once she had took down a few creatures, and stood confidently arms crossed in front of him he soon went on his merry way. She had trapped the remaining escapee corpses in the Covered Market locking the gates with her skeleton key, then sprinted to the next entrance and locked it too. When all three gates on the High Street were done, she climbed the traffic signal jumping onto the semi-circular sign, next onto the window ledges until she reached the roof. She ran across the roof and took a huge leap down onto a van parked on Market Street; she then fell to the street locking the gates this side. The public toilets seemed empty much to River's relief as it would be a shame to spill infected blood on Oxford's most trendy WC's; books and flowers, such a luxury to admire in the city's least expected place. Sprinting on again River cut through Boots' side entrance it was completely empty, save for a few shoplifters who thought Christmas had come early. Out onto Cornmarket Street, River took a left turn heading towards the Golden Cross Shopping Centre sealing off the last entrance.

That was the majority of flesh eating monsters in temporary captivity. River hadn't yet heard from Damien, so her next stop was Boswells. She made her way around to the Broad Street side of the shop where as expected she was greeted by a bin and lamppost to give her a leg up to the first floor window which was open. Being slender she slipped in and made her way down to the chemist. Boswells had become another haven for shoppers and townsfolk. People's emotions were apparent as children were screaming, adults crying and shouting, debating their theories for survival. River walked through them down the stairs to meet Adel the pharmacist, another local friendly face. As usual Adel was being very accommodating to his customers, keeping everyone calm.

"Hey Adel!" River addressed him taking out her ear plugs. "Looks like we have a crisis on our hands."

"Hello River, yes it seems that way, how are you doing?" Adel reminded River a little of Francis Rossi of Status Quo in his appearance.

"Coping, but whatever this disease is it is spreading fast! I need a favour, I have sent refugees to M&S but some will need medical attention, I can see you have your hands full here but have you anyone you can send over – I'll get them there safely," River asked.

"Yes, of course, in fact, I'll come over; we have plenty of trained staff here," Adel offered.

"Great." River walked with Adel towards the Cornmarket Street entrance. "You might want to lock those top windows, I'm not saying they're acrobats but let's not give them the benefit of the doubt," River advised the security guard as they walked out.

The journey over to Queen Street was clear. They reached the entrance safely and Adel went in to attend to the wounded and unsettled.

"Give my best to Ash," Adel said to River – Ash had been a regular to the chemist before his vampiric transition. "Look after yourself," Adel said. Today it had a whole new meaning.

"And you, Adel. Thank you for your help."

River walked through Queen Street towards Bonn Square where she had met Bow earlier this morning, initially planning on a day uncovering the identity of the witch's mystery man. River hated seeing the streets clear, buses abandoned, scared people looking out of the shop windows. Her pity was interrupted by her message tone.

'River, received first victim you enquired about, plus others. Most identified as drug users except one sober victim, rich background. The bloods are coming back with contamination, but no known virus. Police suspect heroin contamination. I'm not convinced. D.'

River texted back; 'Drug users most likely to be found first, get detectives to patrol Jericho and other wealthy areas to either eliminate or identify deaths from different social backgrounds.'

'Will do, will update you when I get anything. D'

River was so angry that as usual it was the people with nothing who were being stripped of their dignity. The blame was always laid with them, based this time on no more evidence than that their bodies were the first to be discovered. If only people could see how their lives actually were they might have a different opinion. It was tempting to let the infection get out of control. To sit by and just let the apocalypse happen. That way people would learn the truth about, survival but the minor point of her sacred duty and also a little compassion for the human race gave her strength to carry on the fight.

A single zombie shuffled his way up the underpass, wearing a rather expensive suit, ripped and bloody, limping, still clutching his suitcase.

River walked over casually, "sorry Mister, I know you didn't come to work today expecting to develop a nasty cold, well perhaps a cold is an understatement, anyway, I'm going to have to borrow that suitcase."

She ducked as the poor dead bloke took a swing for her, grabbing his briefcase she clunked him over the head. He collapsed to the ground his head falling off and rolling down the underpass.

"Pretty," she remarked.

"Pretty gruesome," a voice said from behind her.

"Hey Punk," River greeted. "So where's your ghost friend?"

"Well, her body, is still in the JR, her ghost as you put it, is at my place asleep and safe. I think our priority has changed. This needs to be sorted River; there are already a ridiculous amount of fatalities. Do you know the source yet?" Punk asked.

"No, Damien said there's an unknown pattern in the bloods."

"Yeah, people are going crazy, two coppers were arguing outside the station on the way up. One was adamant it was down to an artefact shown at the Antiques Roadshow last weekend."

"Punk, that's it! I wonder if Christ Church Cathedral still has a list of applicants who had antiques valued. We could try and locate the source!"

"Not a bad plan River, but what if we're wrong?"

"I know what I'll do if it's right!"

"Smashing things isn't always the answer Riv'!'"

"Nah, I know but sometimes, what else can we do? I've got a city of people likely to become infected, a witch with a sacred mission to protect some guy and she doesn't know why, and your ghost girl, so how does smashing things up sound now?" River said without stopping for a breath between her words.

"Yeah, ok girl, no need to get stressed. Anyway tell me about this witch."

"Nosy bugger."

Punk smiled. River was glad to have a familiar face by her side as they headed to the cathedral's office.

"So, any idea where we're going to find any paperwork?" Punk asked delicately.

"Well first we'll check the rooms that say PRIVATE on them; I wouldn't have thought they'd have been filed away in vaults so soon, the Roadshow was quite recent." River said.

"Good plan."

"So I don't suppose you had time to check your books before you came out?"

"I did actually, but nothing we don't already know; decapitation kills them, don't get bitten, don't expect them all to be slow moving, blah blah and so on. And there was a couple of suggestions for sources such as freak viruses, spells, contained curses."

"I think we're on the right track, Punk. I reckon if we get hold of some old thing with a lid and smash it, it will be over – I bet it's a contained curse."

"What about your new witch friend, could she help?"

"Well, I guess, she's pretty good at what she does. But she's wrapped up with her guy, and I think her energy may be best used later."

"Yeah, you're probably right. So what's she like?"

River looked at Punk flatly, "Haven't you already got

some girl living with you, and another bunch chasing you from the Uni?" River tried changing the subject. Punk had been a friend for years. They'd fought together side by side, researched books until early hours in the morning, spent most of their time together, the best of friends. But River was starting to realise her affection for Punk wasn't just a friendly sort of affection, perhaps she'd always thought Punk would never be interested in relationships but now new female attention was catching his eye, it felt like she was losing him.

It was nearly two pm, the day had been swallowed in the mayhem. They walked past Carfax. The blood from this morning's jumper stained the ground but now there was more than a grey pavement painted red. The roads were empty; buses obviously hadn't quite made it to Queen Street. There were odd shoes and bags scattered all over that people had dropped in their panic. Terrified shoppers were looking out of the windows onto the street debating whether their commercial prisons were really safe or if an escape would be worth a try. As Punk and River took a right turn and walked to St Aldates a few abandoned buses and cars were beginning to be seen. Soon the queue of traffic fleeing the city of blood stricken spires was apparent. It wasn't apparent though what sort of commuters the traffic hosted. There didn't seem to be any dead stragglers about, River hoped they were still locked tightly in the Covered Market. Her priority for now was to locate the source of the outbreak; anyone locked in their cars alive should be safe.

They walked quietly until they came to the first entrance to Christ Church, usually off limits to the public.

"It's so eerie," Punk said.

"I know, it's not right," River whispered cautiously.

She put her arm out in front of Punk, and gestured silence with her right finger on her lips.

Shuffling could be heard approaching from the corner, a Christ Church custodian still wearing his navy bowler hat appeared. Flesh had been peeled from his face; his eyes nearly white except for the just about visible pin point pupil. Unexpectedly his elderly shuffle transformed into a near gallop.

"Watch out!" River screamed.

Punk jumped to one side. River ran up the wall and jumped into a roundhouse kick dismantling the head of the zombie keeper.

"Well you have to give it to him – he still was pretty miffed about us using the private entrance!" Punk joked.

River laughed. "C'mon, let's hurry up; if they're coming from in there now then we could be soon walking into a swarm."

There was no room for recklessness as they made their way to the inside of the cathedral's college buildings.

"So are we going to split up or stay together?" Punk asked waiting for instruction.

"Splitting up would save time but we could be wrong, the papers may not even be here and we are walking into a huge risk, I vote we stay together," River replied thoughtfully.

Soon they had kicked down any of the doors that hadn't already been left open, searched through tonnes of paperwork but had no luck.

"It's no good; it can't be here. For all we know it could have been taken home in a briefcase," Punk suggested.

"Hang on, let me try Bow. This may be where she can play a part."

River texted Bow the talented witch, to see if she could do a location spell for the paper work. It wasn't long before Bow had texted back; her magick was powerful and much faster than standard modern witchcraft.

"Follow me, it's in an office in the Old Library," River informed Punk, they were soon at the Old Library and shuffling through paperwork with bloody hands from the numerous corpses they had had to fight on the way – hungry scabby corpses who were ravenous for fresh flesh.

"Got it!" Punk shouted.

"Quick, scan through, is anything there familiar? The photos, do they resemble anything you have seen in books, or the names of any artefacts?"

"I'm looking River but it's all pretty normal boring stuff, nothing that says 'full of flu'. To be honest most of this stuff doesn't look like it could contain anything; we have swords, plates, relics, collections but no vases or pots with lids."

The moans and groans of the increasing number of zombies was both frightening and frustrating. River slammed the office door shut and blocked it with the desk she had effortlessly dragged to barricade it. "I can't hold these much longer, Punk, work with me, or we need to take the list away."

Punk looked up to River. As he glanced at where the desk had been he noticed an urn decorated with ancient drawings sat in an arched indent of the wall. "River, that urn!"

River looked over to it then looked at Punk. Punk grabbed the urn and smashed it to the floor.

Perhaps the noise of the smashed urn startled the corpses but it was soon clear that a curse was not contained inside it as the weight of the door being hammered from outside began again.

"Plan B," River proposed.

"Which is?"

"Get out of here alive and get everyone to safety, we need to inform Ash and Zen. Hospitals are a big 'no' for now, if medical supplies are needed then we hit the supermarkets and head to Dalton Barracks or Brize Norton, but Dalton will be closer."

"River I don't think an army base is the best place, aren't they instructed to shoot to kill in this circumstance, and what if anyone we take over for sanctuary fails a zombie test? Surely there is some way we can look after people until we get to the bottom of this."

"What if we can't get to the bottom of this?" River said glumly.

"Don't think like that. Hey, chin up. If we get through this we'll go out and celebrate just you and me!"

River smiled, though her smile soon faded as her arms weakened nearly failing to hold the desk against the door.

Her text tone sounded, "Take that from my pocket Punk, it might be Damien."

Punk did as River asked and read out the text, "I KNOW THE SOURCE, IT'S NOT A VIRUS, NOR A CONTAINED CURSE JUST THE PETTY POWERDRIVE OF SOME BITCH WITCH I'VE HEARD OF CALLED VESTRA. WE NEED TO COUNTERACT IT. RING ME WHEN A GOOD TIME, I SENSE YOU'RE A BIT STUCK, STAND BACK AND I'LL SEND YOU SOME HOUSEKEEPING. BOW."

"Awesome, I love that girl," River said.

"How did she know?" Punk asked.

"She gets occasional visions when she meditates sometimes; I bet she was able to see the exact situation we are currently in. Get ready to run."

"Why?" Punk enquired. A blast of fire was then visible outside of the door through the small window. "Never mind."

"Come on, we need to try and speak to Bow." River moved the desk and opened the door; they both raced out of the cathedral grounds to safety.

"Light at the end of the tunnel!" River said through a happy sigh.

A temporary fire had illuminated Christ Church College and Cathedral which was enough to put off any walking corpses whilst River phoned Bow with Punk by her side. Both of them a little charred from sprinting away from the burn.

* * *

Bodies lay everywhere, some were rising, others escaped the horrible fate of the fast spreading virus and stayed down. Windows were smashed, blood and corpses were all that could be seen from the once 'Dreaming Spires'. The whole of Oxford, north, east, south and west, displayed the remains of a bloody battle. Larger shops and warehouses were housing people from the dreadful streets. The homeless were the best at survival, life not being much different than usual for them - there was nowhere wholly safe, no one person you could entirely trust and a huge population attacking. It was not a pretty sight when the zombies had managed to reach tourist towers such as St Mary's, Carfax, St George's and St Michael's. People were jumping from the heights to avoid coming face to face with the terrifying mutated creatures. They would fall to the ground twisted and bloody to then be approached by scavengers ripping away at the warm freshly slaughtered meat. Some were hanging onto the external architecture but the zombies still attacked them, feeding from them alive as if they were a hanging treat from a cage. The number was rapidly increasing and it was becoming widely believed that the apocalypse was upon Oxford.

Oxford's slayer stood with her close friend and watcher, Punk.

"Bow has the bits she needs to begin to counteract the spell but it needs four people and a safe place, somewhere undisturbed," River explained to Punk and then continued, "That should be doable."

River took her phone from pocket. "Hi Zen, yeah it's time, we need you – Bow knows what to do but we need two more people and somewhere quiet. We're at County Hall, balancing on the wall to the side where we're kind of attracting a bit of corpse-action-attention. Great. Hurry won't you?" River put the phone in her pocket. "They're on their way. She said the tunnels below the court should be perfect."

Soon Zen and Ash approached under a large umbrella, sheltering from what little sun was actually shining. They threw attacking zombies aside effortlessly as they entered the small forecourt. With one leap they were on the wall with River and Punk.

"Ok, we need to get in there," Ash announced.

They all looked at each other. It was tiring stamping on the fingers of the creatures below that were trying to grab their legs – particularly Punk and River's, the zombies didn't have much interest in the vamps.

Bow, at home in her small bedsit, sat cross legged in front of the mixture of herbs and a lit black candle.

Kneeling up now she surrounded herself and workspace in salt for added protection then called upon the elements represented by candles in their correct compass points.

She focused intently and started with a yellow candle, "Air, you surround us, we breathe you in, we exhale you, I call you to the circle." The breeze in the room was apparent as the curtains flew just as they would have if the window were open.

Next she turned to Spirit, represented by a purple candle, "Spirit, you take us through the worlds, you make us who we are, I call you to the circle." She felt strong, sure of herself and her power.

Next the blue candle, "Water, you cleanse us, cool us and refresh us. I call you to the circle." Her skin felt fresh, as though she had bathed in a crystal blue waterfall.

She carried on turning clockwise to the green candle, "Earth, we come from you, we return to you, our Goddess lives in everything you possess. I call you to the circle." The scent of the plants Bow had in her room passed under her nose as if she had stood and inhaled directly over them.

Finally she shuffled around completing the circle turning her attention to the red candle, "Fire, you give us warmth, you give us strength, you burn away what we no longer need, I call you to the circle." Lighting the last candle, an extension of the warmth from the flame she had just lit gently soared through her. She had the attention of all the elements of which she needed help for her magick to work accurately.

"So where do we come into this?" Zen enquired having now gained access to the tunnels of County Hall.

"Bow said we need to hold hands, make a circle, and focus on how Oxford was before this broke out," River informed. "Oh, we need to chant this incantation too," she showed her friends the words from Bow's text.

They did as Bow had asked.

From her room in her circle of light Bow focused intently on Vestra, the witch she had dreamt about, she summoned her just outside the circle in her room.

Before Bow stood a young witch the same age as her, her hair was like white silk, she wore a burgundy gown. To a stranger unfamiliar to the true strength her charms would make her appear an innocent well-mannered girl.

"So you're the scoundrel who's caused this mess?" Bow asked as the illusion of Vestra smirked before her.

"Beautiful don't you think?" Vestra said. Her voice somewhat high pitched.

"No I don't – and I'm sorry Vestra but it's the last thing you'll ever do to hurt anyone. As we speak my friends are reciting the incantation to counteract your mess, the city is being transformed as if nothing ever happened. No-one will be hurt and no citizen will possess any memory past the second this terror began," Bow explained.

"Silly witch, you need to access my altar to do such," Vestra spat back but soon her face was full of fear as she felt her power being drained. She realised that Bow had not just summoned her but physically transported to her home. Vestra was looking at an astral version of Bow. The good witch destroyed every amulet, urn and tool that could hold the power Vestra had built up. Vestra would soon only be a person, powerless. Her illusion faded as Bow's reappeared in her own room, still protected in her circle.

The candles surrounding Bow extinguished and a sensation of peace was restored in Bow's mind. "Thank you elements, you may leave the circle. Thank you

Goddess, thank you for your guidance." She smiled as she remembered that her earlier prophetic vision of Vestra was not the only dream she had had. Now this crisis was over she remembered what she thought was the destiny of the guy she was sent to protect, and had fallen in love with. But as much as she tried to remember the memory gently floated away. She wasn't disheartened as she realised that it had been an incentive and she would hopefully be able to learn and experience this new destiny for real with a fresh mind. She smiled, incredibly happy.

In just a few minutes of great concentration and focus Vestra had been taken down and the sun shone over the spires and roof tops of Oxford. River, Punk, Zen and Ash awakened from the trance Bow had gently sent them into. They all smiled realising that they had been successful in helping her. By the time they had reached the surface it was apparent, peering from the shadows, that not one person of the general public was any the wiser of the living nightmare they had just experienced.

A man stood at the top of Carfax tower, gazing into the sun. His clothes were torn and dirty, his stubble looked rough, and his hair overgrown. He did not know why he was stood at the top of the tower so he made his way back to the ground. As he made his way down the lady at the ticket office nodded and smiled at him. He smiled back. Just a few steps out into the street a well dressed lady, around the same age as him, maybe a year younger, approached him.

"You look lost; I live not far from here and was looking for someone to flat share with, it's rent free. What do you think?" She surprised herself by asking but her feelings overcome any doubt.

"That would be lovely, thank you," he said. They walked off together unknowing that they would start a new life together with a happy ending.

Something was in the air of Oxford, people weren't taking their lives for granted and kindness circled, everyone looked at one another with a little more respect and happiness was tangible.

Him

He was neither dead nor alive. Though he didn't even realise, he just went on being busy, 'working and doing other stuff,' he would tell people. He wasn't a vampire, or a ghost, in fact nothing of the kind. He was probably once a human, maybe something better or perhaps nothing at all. He had no memories of his past. He cared for some people, although he wasn't obvious about it. He was stuck in a daily routine with little change: a walk up St Aldate's, coffee, speaking to many of the passers-by as he worked. He knew the city well, but he didn't know of the ghosts, vampires, witches, warlocks and demons who passed him every day. Someone cared about him he knew, but he was too wrapped up in fading away from existence to care. There was still time for him to be saved but he wasn't strong enough to let anyone come close enough to do so. The gargoyles watched over him. They had been told to shield him. To anyone else he appeared worthless, he was in fact very valuable, but only the Higher Powers knew why. Everyone else had their role to protect him.

The young witch, Bow, felt great rage towards him, even though deep down she was in love with him. It hadn't been that long ago that she had realised she was even a witch. She had prayed to the Gods and Goddesses all her life, always believing in them. Before her magick had become apparent she had lived a fairly normal life for a twenty-something year old. She stopped counting her years now that she felt she was getting older rapidly. Magick was her life, studying it and embracing it in her small abode. Her two-way connection with the Higher Powers was the most important thing to her. She knew that humans were not alone in the city. She hadn't needed to be told nor did she need evidence to convince her, it was something she just knew. Just like the message she had been given by the Goddess wasn't the pen and paper kind, more the 'bump into a guy and know your life's duty is to protect him' kind. The dreams didn't help her ignore her destiny either. She tried so hard to leave him to dig his own grave with his stupidity. That's how she knew it wasn't just a silly crush. Frustratingly, no matter how hard she tried to keep him out of her mind she found herself bumping into him more often and in time feeling stronger about him. She tried to explore her feelings but he wasn't interested. One day he would smile but another day he'd just blank her. She loathed him when he was hot and cold, the tennis of emotions in her mind was driving her insane. She asked the Goddess over and over, all she would get back was 'be patient'. She took vows in prayer once she realised her duty and tried to fulfil it the best she could. She knew he was special, she just didn't know why. Perhaps if the Higher Powers wouldn't answer her questions she would need to find answers elsewhere. She would go in search of those other worldly creatures, anyone who might know more about this guy. She was also sure there was a slayer. A few location spells should do the trick; at least it would take her mind off of him for a while.

* * *

"Hey!" she said reluctantly to him, he made her feel sixteen again.

"You alright?" he returned as a greeting, she didn't think he cared much whether she was or not.

"So, I keep bumping into you," she tried to make conversation.

"Well, you know, I kind of work here," he looked ill at ease.

"Right, so what're you selling?" Scraping for something to talk about, she silently grinded her teeth, embarrassed.

He raised his arm no more than an inch gesturing her to look at the magazine in his hand.

"Oh cool, so some sort of tourist magazine?"

"That's right," he thought maybe he should offer a little interest. "*The Big Issue* was getting hard to sell. A local writer released a tourist mag for vendors trying to find their feet, that way the Issue could be sold solely by the homeless, or that's what I gather anyway."

"That was a good idea, so you're trying to find your way in life?" Bow asked. He looked like he was happy with his current lifestyle, which she speculated she knew but wouldn't let on.

He smiled, thinking the same as her. "Something like that," he said. There was a brief silence.

"Ok, so I better get on," he added. He regretted making conversation, because she was lingering now.

She really wanted to move off, but couldn't. "Right, so maybe see you again?"

"I expect so," he offered.

"You usually about here?"

"Here and there, we're allowed to choose our own spots, so ..."

"Right," she said. She was still trying to move on. "Hey, look I've been so rude; let me buy one from you," she said and reached into her bag. She had had a small win on the lottery which meant she was ok for money; a tenner should be worth the five minutes of his time she felt she had wasted. She handed it him and said, "I would say keep the magazine but maybe it will be worth a read?"

"Perhaps," he said as he took the note. "Appreciate it, thanks."

"Right, walk on Bow," she instructed herself.

"Bow?" he questioned.

"My name, short for Boudica, well it's my middle name actually, my first name is Anne, but I fancied an unusual nickname."

He raised an eyebrow.

"Yes so, I'm off," she said as she realised she was rambling on.

He pursed his lips, shifting his glance until she went. At least she hadn't turned out to be a complete time waster, he thought. Strange, she seemed to be hanging around a lot lately; maybe she wasn't quite all 'there' or had some strange obsession. Oh well, she had gone.

* * *

Wow, that was awkward. Why hadn't she just resisted and gone on to find the slayer, it was like some magnet drew her there. She felt a little warmer on the surface toward him but she was a little uncomfortable with how she had just acted. Brush it off, she thought, concentrate on ignoring him and just get on with your job, he doesn't need to know about you. But she wanted him to.

* * *

The day had been long, she couldn't find the slayer, the location spell she had done was incorrect by the time she had made small talk with him. She went to all the spots she thought she might be patrolling but no luck and now it was getting dark. Which graveyard was a slayer likely to be hanging about in? Somewhere with recent graves perhaps? Both St Giles and St Mary Magdalen always had that eerie feeling, though the graves were too old to be dusting new vamps and there were no mausoleums either that Bow knew of. Rose Hill Cemetery on Church Cowley Road seemed a good bet. It took about an hour's dawdle to reach it from the city centre. She didn't mind, she was hoping she might bump into him again, and if not she was enjoying reminiscing from the morning. She held tightly to the magazine she had bought from him. As she reached the cemetery she realised the gates were closed, she shut her eyes after a good look at the other side and visualised being inside the cemetery. It wasn't the most complex magick she had performed and within seconds she was in.

"Excuse me Miss, I wondered if you could help me out? I was tending to my aunt's grave and must have missed the groundkeeper locking the gates. Do you know another way out?" asked a trendy looking man wearing a brown hoody and dull blue jeans.

'Yeah, you look the sort that would rush down just before closing to tend to your aunt's grave,' Bow thought sarcastically.

"Leave her alone, vamp!" another voice behind the dead man walking emerged.

A slim, dark haired girl became visible as she neared them, stake in her hand, walking confidently.

"You must be the slayer?" Bow enquired.

"That's right, who's asking?" she replied.

"Give me a second." Bow closed her eyes again for a matter of seconds, the fire materialized at the vamps feet spreading upwards until he burnt into a mound of ash.

"A witch, nice," the slayer remarked.

"Yeah, though not the oracle," Bow returned.

"So that's why you're here, in search of me? In search of answers I'd hazard a guess?"

"You wouldn't be wrong."

"Fire away, though not literally."

Bow let out a little laugh; at least the slayer had a sense of humour. "So, I'm not sure what your take is on the Higher Powers?"

"I'm open minded, kind of handy in my line of work."

"Right, so I've got to protect a guy, he's actually under seriously heavy guard, a whole network, gargoyles, angels..."

"Witches, yeah I get the picture."

"I don't know why I have this job though, I mean he's kind of hot but a little self involved, possibly on drugs. He doesn't have much of a life put it that way."

"And you've fallen for him?"

"I never said I'd fallen for him!" Bow defended.

"You didn't need to sugar, kind of blushing there."

"Right, so anyway ... I want to know why he's worth my time, especially as he seems really unfriendly and only particularly fond of small talk."

"Maybe he's shy?"

Bow burst out a huge laugh. "He is not shy, just well a little of the 'I don't want nor need friends' attitude."

"Ok, human?" the slayer quizzed.

"I've talked to him like once, maybe twice, I don't know his life story."

The slayer raised her eyebrows at Bow, arms crossed.

"I got the impression he's human," Bow concluded.

"What makes you think he's an addict?" the slayer quizzed.

"Instinct, plus some other local guys said that was his deal."

"He's not, if this guy is so precious there is no way fate would have taken him down that road."

"Oh." Bow, felt a little stupid for making that assumption and especially on the basis of street gossip.

"OK, I'll see what I can do. In return you can do me a favour."

Bow kept eye contact with the slayer, waiting for her proposition.

"Be part of my standby team, you'd be kind of useful."

"Yeah cool. How do you contact me?"

The slayer took her mobile from her trousers. "Take my number," she said.

Bow typed in the number to her own mobile. "What name do you go by?"

"River."

"Cool name, I'm Bow."

"Good," River replied. "Now let's see what we can find out about this guy. Meet me tomorrow morning in the city centre; see if you can point him out. We could go for a drink after and I'll brief you on things you could help me out with."

"Sounds fine. Let's meet behind the monument on

Bonn Square, I think we should be inconspicuous."

"Ok, sometime around ten," River concluded.

"Hey, slayer!" voices from the deeper end of the cemetery called out.

"See you then River," Bow said as River casually walked into the darkness toward the approaching vamps.

Bow walked home to her bedsit. She couldn't sleep that night, every time she drifted off curiosity woke her and endless thoughts prevented her from switching off. She would be glad when it was ten o'clock tomorrow morning. She was a little excited about being acquainted with the local slayer, not only might she make a friend, but she might also put her gifts to use. Then there was him. She might, at last, be on her way to uncovering his mask, either that or being thrown from the job. It didn't matter; she was dedicated now to protecting him from harm, no matter who or what was in her way.

* * *

Bow somehow felt that she was actually more conspicuous trying to be inconspicuous. Maybe it was just because she felt guilty trying to find out about this guy. She sat on one of the newly placed benches near the top of

Bonn Square. She remembered the only vivid dream she had managed to sleep through last night.

Dreams were always random, and this one followed suit. She was walking back home from the cemetery, but somehow ended up in the city. There wasn't a single vehicle, person or being in sight. The centre was dead. Panic suddenly filled her like she had lost something precious, something irreplaceable. She ran everywhere in desperation, then she gave up. She sat in the centre of Gloucester Green, cross-legged, head in hands, like a mad person, talking to herself, recalling her trail. Someone placed a hand on her wrist gently. She looked up cautiously, and she saw him. The panic drained smoothly as she had found what she had lost. She explained the nightmare to him.

"I tried to lose you but it was awful, like damnation, I wanted to leave you to your own free will but they punished me, I thought the Higher Powers were kind. Why have they made me do this? I can't look after you," she confessed.

He didn't say anything. She looked scared. He knelt down in front of her stroking her hair; he gained her trust as he looked gently into her frightened eyes. Lightly raising her chin, his lips met hers caressing, teasing her into a soft kiss. He parted slowly, checking her reaction before he pressed his lips deeper on hers into a moment of passion.

Bow came crashing back to earth in realisation. She remembered what had happened when he had kissed her; his destiny had been revealed to her but it was blurry now. Had that been the result of the Higher Powers, her power, or maybe some telepathic link to him?

"Bow," River had arrived, "you look confused."

"I just remembered some dream I had last night, I think I got some insight into why he's so special."

"Well I did some research, he's known about, some think he is a demi-god or something but I don't think that is the case. He's certainly got the attention around here, but he sure doesn't know it. We need to work out what his deal is and fast, something's not right," River paused. "Bow, I'm really sorry, I feel something's not right, let me go and check it out and we'll meet up again soon. Hey, maybe go back home and see if you can get any more psychic dreams!"

River ran to the top of Queen Street, as she expected, she was greeted by a crowd, the police and a twisted body lying on the street in front of Carfax tower.

* * *

River had been cautious walking into the graveyard, it crossed her mind it could be a vamp nest she was walking into. Then she had caught sight of Punk.

"What are you doing here?" she asked, surprised.

"You texted me, woman," he replied.

"What?"

"Look," he pulled his phone from his pocket and flashed the message display at her: 'Meet me at Iffley Church, midnight.'

River looked at him confused, "Show me the message details."

Punk brought them up on the screen; it was definitely her number, 23:05.

"I was asleep then, jerk. How could I've sent it?"

"Well, I don't know, in your sleep, anyway what are you doing here?"

"I don't know, I had a kind of slayer dream, thought I should check it out."

"So, what's the urgency?" Bow was walking down the churchyard path to the outdoor font where she saw River and a slightly taller, muscular guy.

"She sent you a text too?" Punk enquired.

"Yes, why don't you recall doing so?" Bow replied.

"No, I was just telling Punk, I woke from a dream that guided me here."

"Slayerrrr!" Ash shouted appearing from the right side of the church with Zen.

"So what's the deal?" Zen asked.

"Sorry, is there anyone else I called to my side, how the hell could I have texted all of you with my eyes closed?"

"Maybe you didn't," Bow offered.

"Excuse skipping introductions, but you're the witch right in with the Higher Powers?" Punk asked Bow.

"That's right, anything else you know about me?" Bow said defensively.

"Allow me, Bow. This is Punk, my friend who's pretty good at researching stuff, my unofficial watcher. Zen is a fallen angel turned vampire who sired Ash. Ash is her companion and they have given me their oath to leave the good folk alone, and clean up the streets of murderers and the like. Everyone, this is Bow, my new friend and witch, don't hack her off as she's pretty good at what she does. Everyone knows each other now? Great, now can we figure out how and why I unwittingly gathered you all here?"

"Sooo... what I was going to say was, if Bow is working for them upstairs and you didn't send us a text, perhaps we have been called by the bosses?" Punk concluded. "Oh and thanks for saving our skin in that little zombie crisis," he added quietly to Bow.

"Only one way to find out why we're here," Zen proposed.

"Yes, but keep holy articles to yourselves please!" Ash added.

River walked to the door and read the notice to herself:

THE CHURCH IS OPEN TO VISITORS
DURING THE DAY.

"I expect it is locked," River assessed.

"It's not anymore," Bow confessed.

"Impressive," Ash remarked.

"Don't get excited, you still need an invite to enter people's homes," River added.

"If I wanted to I could have kicked the door open, I was just making a comment," Ash said guardedly.

"So are we actually going to go in or just stand here and redundantly discuss the many ways of opening a door?" Punk was getting a little impatient. He wasn't a people person at the best of times, even if he was popular, but waiting outside a church on a cold dark night with a bunch of supernatural beings wasn't his idea of fun.

"Just be on your guard," River warned.

Ten minutes had passed as the little group stood outside the church. River pushed the door carefully. Nothing jumped out, but she wasn't convinced it was safe.

"We need to get this place lit up," River whispered lighting candles around the chapel.

Ash and Zen spread wide from each other keeping guard for any nasty surprises whilst River pulled a light from her pocket and began lighting some of the church's many candles.

"Here let's help River," Punk took two lighters from his denim waistcoat pocket and handed one to Bow.

The chapel was magnificent; a huge font stood before them a few feet from the door. To one side of the font were raised pews rounding the corner, whilst opposite a huge organ stood. Rows of pews led to the front of the church. It reminded Bow of a medieval chapel. Slightly separated at the front of the chapel was a large altar with a very large cross which Ash and Zen found slightly intimidating.

As the group cast their eyes around the church many memorial plaques, chandeliers and stained glass windows caught their attention.

"Not that this church isn't spectacular, but why would your dream send a group of the most unlikely suspects to a Christian place of worship?" Bow enquired.

The outer wooden side door of the chapel opened, a cast iron gate stood between the outer door and the church. Everyone's eyes went straight to the door. A hooded figure appeared, closing the chapel door behind him. Positioning themselves in readiness for battle the group watched as the gate swung open. The hooded figure glided through. Bow and Punk exchanged a look of terror, having a little less courage than the other three.

"No need to panic my little warriors. I come with a message not a threat," said the hooded figure. He had the appearance of a monk. His robe's hood rested very low over his face leaving only his mouth visible.

He did not walk but glided a foot above the floor until he was in front of them.

"Thank you for letting me borrow your mind earlier River. It takes much time and effort to transmit more than one dream at a time so the convenience of modern technology amongst you kids these days proved useful. Now let us get down to it as they say."

No one said anything; the shock of a ghost monk calling a gathering to a church in the middle of the night was still a little difficult to grasp, not to mention his hypnotic use of modern technology.

"Well don't worry, I don't bite. Though that can't be said for everyone now can it?" he laughed a jovial chuckle and placed a huge book on the font. "Firstly I'll make a note of all those present, no, no, I shall do that later. I have a message from the Higher Powers. They are very pleased with your work overall. And although they were a little disappointed with Zen's rebellion, they are quite pleased that Ash has proved his worth. Bow, you know curiosity did kill the cat, patience, patience. And that brings us nicely onto the next point: you were all, or nearly all, born to become Oxford's protectors. You must all work together through your lives to keep Oxford's buildings and citizens from harm. Dark forces are becoming 'ill-contained' and it's up to you to deal with them. In return the Higher Powers will reward you with eternal life; you will not age nor die, and your skills will thrive. You may find others like yourselves are sent to join you over time, welcome them, and fight by their sides. I shall be available to guide you when you are desperate for help, but remember I am just a messenger, I do not know all. Everyone following so far?" the monk asked.

"So let me get this straight, you're some messenger from the Gods and we've been written into time to protect this city, in exchange for being superheroes? Sounds sorted to me, bruv," Punk summarised for everyone.

"Yes that is about the long and short of it," the monk concluded.

"Look I don't want to be impatient and I'm grateful for this calling, but if we're to be working for the Higher Powers I think I have the right to know why they brought that guy to my attention," Bow demanded.

"Yes, I was just coming to that," the monk replied. "As always, there is a catch. The 'guy' you are referring to is the source of all your power. He is 'the sorcerer' and I don't mean of the warlock variety. If he comes to any harm your power will weaken. And if he does not learn of his place soon, he will fade from existence."

"So why was this Bow's battle to begin with?"

"What will concern you all is for Bow to discover with him. Things don't always have to be grim!"

Bow's eyebrows raised and head bowed in embarrassment as she realised the monk was indicating that some benefit for the group would be initiated if she were to get involved with the now not so mysterious guy.

Zen and River both smiled at Bow.

"I feel so many girly chats coming on!" River said.

Punk cleared his throat in embarrassment at talk of romance.

"Moving on," the monk broke the atmosphere. "Stick together, check in with me now and then and most importantly watch your backs. I am to give you all a medallion pendant each; by accepting this you accept your duty."

The medallions were silver, about the size of a two-pound coin. Bow examined hers proudly; on one side was a skyline of Oxford circling the rim, on the reverse angel wings. Each medallion had their individual name inscribed. The medallions hung from a sealed thick brown leather chord, which was long enough to hang over their chests.

"How do we find you if we need you?" River enquired.

"Any church or chapel in Oxford, you simply call my name, as long as you are wearing your medallion."

"And what might your name be?" Ash queried.

"Why, Brother Oxford, of course. And now I bid you all a good night," the monk bowed his head and dematerialised before them.

"Right, ok. Just another normal night in the world of weird then," Punk observed.

"So I want to know how you're going to increase our powers," Zen teased Bow as they all walked from the chapel.

"Yeah, let's not go there," Bow replied.

"Why not?" River asked.

"Because I'm no match for him."

"Don't be silly; give it time, and a bit of witchcraft," Punk joined in, a little easier now.

"Yeah, once he realises you're not too bad beneath those baggy garments you wear, I'm sure he won't be so unwilling," Ash offered.

"Um, have you been spying on me?" Bow enquired.

"Well, not intentionally, just happened to be walking past one night, and well thought I'd see who you were so I could say 'hi' when I bumped into you," Ash admitted.

"Liar," Zen remarked.

"None of your actual business, until you're introduced," Bow tried to avoid the previous analysis from her friends.

"Oh nice tattoo by the way, ouch."

"Oh ok, that is way too much information about my own personal life for tonight, thanks," Bow said mortified.

"So, maybe start with coffee?" River suggested.

"Yeah, let's just worry about the freaky monk for tonight," Punk tried to save what dignity Bow felt she had left.

"Yeah, leave her alone guys, anyway when we all suddenly feel super powerful we'll know why," Zen winked at Bow.

"If we must discuss this then it's going to have to be over a very large scrumpy in the Turf Tavern, and not tonight, I'm beat," Bow said in a final attempt.

They walked out of the village bantering and laughing until they had to go their separate ways.

Bow was looking forward to dreaming, even just laying awake thinking. She was falling for him, but she didn't even know his name, stupid life she thought, but really she loved every minute of it.

River had told everyone to take it easy for a couple of days and let all the revelations sink in. The mix of a zombie crisis was enough in itself, but they also had to accept their calling to an eternal destiny and now lend their energies towards creating a perfect spirit world for Punk's ghost girl Louisa, and her lover, Blake to rule over. Everyone was keen to take some time enjoying the city, a little patrolling if necessary but no major mission work. It was over a year since Ash had been turned into a vampiric angel by Zen, a month since the walking dead invasion and initiation of Oxford's protectors; though they still hadn't agreed on a satisfying name for their mini army.

October 2014

Bow strolled up the High Street early on a fine October morning. She cut through Queens Lane heading towards Broad Street. A loud whistle stopped her as she walked under The Bridge of Sighs. She looked up to see River standing on the rooftop of the Bodleian Library.

"Come on up it's amazing!" River shouted down.

Bow stared intently at the rooftop for a few seconds and was soon standing at River's side.

"Well either that spell didn't quite work or I'm suffering vertigo!"

"A witch who doesn't like heights, that's kind of ironic," River said in amusement.

"It's not like I fly on a broom, anyway better a witch than a slayer if one of us is to have issues with altitude," Bow defended.

"True," River said. "I love it up here, looking down on the Radcliffe Camera and Hertford Bridge."

"It is beautiful, and hey, we have eternity to admire this mind blowing city."

River laughed, "Maybe enough time to cure your dizziness, there is so much to admire. So what were you doing in town so early?"

"Just, well gathering my thoughts."

"You're thinking about him aren't you?"

Bow shrugged her shoulders, and gazed at the street below.

River put her hand on Bow's shoulder, "Guys huh, pain in the—"

"Yeah, kind of. It's like, one minute I'm really happy thinking about him, relating to song lyrics as I listen to the music, then just one little negative thought crosses my mind and I'm plunged into dark thoughts. I've exhausted the power in my laptop writing diary entries, anything to put my energy into something other than him. I've cut myself off from life and now there is all this pressure because everyone is curious about what the monk at Iffley

Church meant. I've actually been avoiding him, River, because I'm scared."

"What are you scared of Bow?"

"Rejection, time wasting, shall I go on?"

"Might sound a little obvious but can't you do a spell?"

"If it's meant to be River it will be. I can't interfere in the power of the universe just to make myself happy."

"I guess," River said, lost for positive suggestions.

"Sorry Riv, I'm spreading the down energy right?"

"No, you're fine girl. I think you should try and talk to him though. Look if you don't want to use your magick what about asking them for a little help upstairs? It's all in their plan right? It sounds to me as though you don't know if you love him or loath him, you crave him and then mourn him. Go and be confident, I'll stick around the rooftops, you know as kind of moral support."

"Thanks Riv. I guess I'll go and 'be confident'."

Bow was soon back on the ground on her way passing the Sheldonian Theatre and pacing through Broad

Street. She stopped at the cobbled cross in the centre of the road, knelt down and placed a white rose she had materialised on the spot as a mark of respect for those burnt at the stake.

"Hey, Bow right?" A voice startled her. Her heart nearly stopped as she looked up to see him.

He stood above her as she knelt on the ground. He was a similar build to Ash, pale and handsome, but a little rough round the edges with messy hair and a little stubble, ripped jeans and fingerless gloves.

'Goddess please help me out here!' Bow silently thought.

"Oh hi, haven't seen you around for a while; was thinking about you," she replied.

"Oh, really?" he asked. He sounded warmer today and a little surprised.

All the things Bow had decided would be acceptable to say to him when she was blasting music at home seemed a whole world away right now.

"So what are you doing in town so early?" Bow asked.

"I'm not sure really, fancied a walk. I feel I should be asking you what you're doing," he smiled.

The conversation seemed to be flowing and the barrier in Bow's head dropped a little.

"I kind of got the impression you thought I was an oddball anyway, so it might not surprise you if I tell you I was laying down a flower as a mark of respect. You know some Martyr's were burnt at the stake here, just for belonging to the wrong religion according to their king. Imagine the pain and fear they must have felt."

He looked thoughtful, "I agree. It's quite poetic, to see a witch laying a rose on the ancient site of a stake."

"How did you know I was a witch?" Bow panicked; surely she hadn't let that slip on their first meeting.

"Wait, I thought you told me?"

"As much as I rambled on that one occasion we talked, I'm pretty sure I didn't tell you."

"You're not denying it though?"

"Look, it's amazing talking to you, but I'm a little confused – last time we talked I got the impression I was wasting your time, and today..?"

"No, I, well, you got me thinking last time, it would be nice to see you again and then I didn't. Then, this might sound strange, but I kept having these weird dreams, and then I come out for a walk and here you are – Hey! Are you pulling some sort of witchcraft on me?"

"No, but you know there was a reason I was keen to talk to you that day. Perhaps we should go somewhere quiet to talk." She looked at him and his presence once again overwhelmed her, especially as she looked into his eyes.

"Walk with me, we'll find somewhere quiet but I don't think I can wait to hear what you have to tell me," he said.

Bow looked up to the top of Blackwell's Art Store to see River leaning on the Iron Man Sculpture, putting two thumbs up. Bow smiled and said, "You know, I can't really tell you, you wouldn't believe me. I'm going to have to show you, but we need to go somewhere really quiet with no interruptions."

"OK, any ideas?" he asked with a little concern in his tone.

"Most places will be opening to staff, and commuters are coming into the city, I'm not sure," Bow thought aloud.

They walked down Turl Street, towards Brasenose Lane and through Radcliffe Square.

Bow's desperate thinking was interrupted by Ash cornering a young looking lad in St Mary's Passage against the church. He was pointing his finger at him; "It's not worth it kid, you think you're big and tough now because they've led you into it. But you know what; you're a joke to them, a little runner, earning their cash! And that shit is going to be amazing for the first couple of hits but then you will crave it and be so ill and ravenous for it. So I'll make you a deal, you run off back to where you came from and get a life and I won't kill you now. If I see you running around for those lowlife addict users again I will destroy you... just to spare you a life of nothingness."

The kid couldn't have been older than eighteen.

"Nice approach Ash," Bow commented as the boy sprinted off looking terrified.

Ash turned around, his fangs exposed, eyes red. He faded to his human face as he saw Bow had company.

Ash and Bow exchanged a look of awkwardness.

"Is this what you wanted to show me?" Bow's guy said.

"Well that was unintentional but, yeah, I guess kind of worth you seeing. I want to show you inside my mind; but as you haven't run already, I've got a feeling you are already unconsciously aware and you've been hiding from this for a while, right?"

He looked to the floor, guiltily and mumbled, "I had a feeling, but I also felt like I was going crazy. I feel like I've been going through some changes. A month or so ago I didn't really care for much, then weird things started happening. It started with the dreams, then you being around, and well, I suppose I'm still battling with myself, trying to figure myself out. That's why I came out; I was looking for you Bow."

Ash looked a little uncomfortable, "I think I'm going to leave you two too it. See ya later Bow." He walked off onto Radcliffe Square.

"If I open up to you do you promise not to turn your back on me?" Bow asked him.

He looked in doubt until he caught her eyes. He hated to admit it to himself but he felt like he cared about her and he sort of owed it to her to make this promise... "As long as you don't turn your back on me."

Bow smiled and said, "First tell me your name; you know it's really awkward referring to you as 'Him' all the time!"

"You talk about me?"

"Don't change the subject."

"I don't know."

"What?"

"I don't know my name, I don't know where I come from; I just seemed to turn up one day, no memories, nothing."

"Kind of figures," Bow thought aloud. "Perhaps it's not important for now. I think what is though, is enrolling you – we might need to visit a church."

"Will this one do?" he asked and indicated the church behind them.

"Absolutely, I love this church, it seems fitting," Bow smiled at the recognition of the silent bond that was forming between him and her.

Bow tried to avoid too much eye contact as they reached the doors of St Mary's. She had a copy of River's skeleton key. Her hand was shaking as she turned it in the lock. Something felt different, the newness and nervousness of a first date, but this moment was completely unanticipated and definitely unexpected. As they walked into the church a sense of peace and security was apparent. The aroma of incense still lingered and the emptiness of the majestic building set an enchanting atmosphere.

"Perhaps we could talk before we get all 'mission-to-save-the-city?" she suggested.

He smiled, and leant his head to the side, beckoning her to find a seat. They walked to a side-facing pew.

"I don't get why you were so closed off when I first met you properly?" she asked.

"I just, well, I didn't get it. I liked you, but I had woken up one day and I knew what I did for a living, I knew the city, but everything else was blank. I recognised you but I didn't know how, so I was wary. I thought I was in some sort of weird dream and if I could just fade away I might wake up. But then of course I began to realise I was awake and my dreams were no ordinary dreams. They were directing me to you, but not only to you, I saw your friend – the vampire? And then there was another dream, a really vivid one of some weird meeting in a church with a monk. I do like you Bow, I just, I don't know if I'm losing it or going in the right direction," he said and looked her in the eyes.

"Imagine how I felt then when I walked past you and felt like I'd been struck by lightning, maybe Zeus was behind it, whatever, I looked at you once, I think I fell in love with you in that second I looked into your eyes. Then I talked with you and I hated you all at the same time as melting with excitement. To cut a long story short I was given the dreams too, told to protect you. It seems you're really special, someone up there likes you!" Bow felt like she had known this guy forever, even though her heart was racing, she also felt completely comfortable talking to him.

"Why?" he asked.

"I don't know, perhaps you were born to be ... The thing is, the Higher Powers, well they seem pretty fond of Oxford, and a calling has been, well called, a group of protectors, given eternal life to keep this city safe." Bow explained feeling a little sacred.

"Where do I come into it?" he questioned.

"Well all I know is that you're like our power source. Brother Oxford, this monk dude, is kind of the messenger to the Gods and that's pretty much all he told us."

"That's right," a voice said.

"WAAH!" Both girl and guy jumped, she grabbed his hand, feeling a surge of ultimate power, her magick apparent in her veins.

Next to him sat the hooded figure.

"I thought I'd wait until we had the real deal here and explain the rest. Oh and I also forgot to mention that you literally only had to say my name in the church and I shall appear!"

"Did you have to give us a heart attack?" Bow said sarcastically.

Brother Oxford stood up and bowed to him and said, "Your Majesty."

Bow looked a little puzzled at a dead monk worshipping a street guy.

"Once a human, but instead of dying you were not reincarnated into new life, instead made by the Gods into the ultimate weapon - a human carrying a source of strength and power for the warriors of Oxford. Simply able to exist forever in the same image as we see you now, the bonus being that your power comes with hidden wonders that you will discover as time goes on. Welcome to your destiny, Raven."

Bow looked a little overwhelmed by the hidden power this guy was apparently distributing unknowingly.

"Raven?" he questioned.

"Your name, sir, is Raven." Brother Oxford informed.

"So that's why I have no memories and have been able to see things at night in my dreams?" Raven asked.

"Indeed, and now you are aware of the power you wield you will grow and thrive as one of Oxford's protectors," the monk explained.

"So he's some sort of demi-god?" Bow enquired.

"Not exactly... demi-gods are conceived. Raven was recycled with extra energy and a fixed age, the only being who ever has been. Raven, you are what the Higher Powers are calling a sorcerer. This means as well as being a source of power, you can physically enhance people's abilities and your own. But take caution and do not be greedy with your power. You will tire if you take too much on too fast and if you tire so will your allies. I take it you accept your sacred duty Raven?" Brother Oxford asked.

Raven looked at Bow; she smiled and gave him an encouraging nod.

"Count me in," Raven agreed.

Brother Oxford, held up a medallion, placing it over Raven's neck. "Don't take it off," he said.

"I won't," Raven promised.

"And now, I bid thee both soul bound a good day," Brother Oxford said and disappeared into the air.

"Soul bound?" Bow questioned quietly.

Raven felt alive, no longer lost, as if the placing of the medallion had initiated something inside, he looked at Bow. Firmly placing his palm around the back of her head, feeling her soft choppy hair, he kissed her. He knew who he was and he knew he was in love with her. An explosion of red light shone brightly lighting the dark church. He looked at her absolutely adoringly and confident. She could see a change in him and feel a change in herself.

"Come on, there's fun to be had before we have work tonight!" he said.

"Hold my hands," Bow said. "Visualise where you want to go."

He held her hands strongly, closed his eyes and imagined holding her, sheltering her in an embrace as they looked at the view of the city from just below St Mary's spire.

"You know I was afraid of heights this morning," Bow remembered, as she now leaned on the barrier of the tower, holding his arms that he had placed around her.

"There's nothing you need be afraid of now," he assured.

River texted Zen and Punk, 'Is it me or do I suddenly feel a lot stronger?'

Zen replied, "Not just you, Ash saw Bow with 'him' heading to St Mary's."

'Bingo, pub for lunch?' River replied.

'You bet,' Zen and Punk texted back.

It was as if being awoken from amnesia. Even though there was still certainty of not recalling knowing each other before, Bow and Raven were besotted with one another. The world had a different light upon it but nothing was as crystal clear as one another.

"There's so much to see, so much ground unexplored, Raven!" Bow turned to Raven, still in their embrace.

"Then we shall uncover it together."

A soft breeze circled them; they enjoyed it, feeling the connection to the Higher Powers, acknowledging their satisfaction.

Holding her hands over his was like nothing Bow had ever felt before. It wasn't just the magickal power inside of him, but the realisation of the affection she had felt for him. A person who she would share her life with forever, a certainty that love would never leave them and that every day would be as wonderful as this. There was no higher comfort than feeling the warmth of his body wrapped around her, his arms wanting to hold her near to him to feel the same comfort.

Bow's phone sounded a notification; she took it out of her pocket. Raven held her, still.

'I hear you pulled! Nice, celebration in the Four Candles babe!' Punk had texted.

'So, I'm hoping it hasn't been posted on Facebook just yet?' Bow texted back.

"This kind of sucks but my friends want to meet up, to, urgh, 'celebrate'," Bow said, a little disappointed but also excited.

"Isn't it a little early for the pub to be open?" he queried.

"Yeah, but one of Zen's old friends Laura is a bar maid and we get served early."

Raven smiled, "It'd be pretty cool to meet your friends, though I'm guessing I'll recognise a couple of them. I've had this feeling that I'm being watched now and then."

Bow laughed.

"So you're sure?" Bow turned around to face him, no fear of falling like she would have had only just this morning.

Their lips locked and as they jointly visualised the pub on George Street the floor adjusted below them from St Mary's tower to the smooth pavement before 'The Four Candles'.

River and Punk approached the pub to see Bow with her man; his blackish silver hair spiked perfectly, his fingerless gloves tucked under his denim jacket with his arms around Bow's shoulders. She was smiling, glowing. He was looking down into her eyes. It was as if they were silently talking to one another.

"Hello!" Punk broke the moment. River nudged him with her elbow. "Ouch."

River rolled her eyes.

"Hi guys," Bow said turning her head to face them.

River noticed Bow had her hands in the back pockets of his jeans. She sucked her cheeks in trying to prevent herself from grinning thinking it was really sweet. "So this is ...?" she asked.

"Meet Raven, and Raven, this is River, Oxford's slayer, and Punk, her kind of watcher," said Bow.

Raven moved his left hand around Bow's back, holding her tightly. With his right he shook both River and Punk's hands, "Nice to meet you," he said; his voice was notably soft and friendly.

A slim, girl with short fiery red dyed hair opened the

door. "Come on in guys," she said smiling.

"Thanks Laura," River said.

Bow and Raven glanced at each other, blind with love they walked into the bar after Punk and River.

Zen smiled standing at the bar, "I remember that incredible feeling, the realisation of a dream."

Ash pouted at her, "What do you mean 'you remember'?!"

"Ash and Zen, meet Raven," River introduced.

"How are you doing chap?" Raven said to Ash.

"You two know each other?" Zen enquired.

"No, remember I told you, Raven saw me grilling that kid this morning," Ash reminded her.

"Nice to meet you Raven, seems as though I'm the last," Zen said.

"Great, I'll sort out drinks and we can have a little chat," Punk announced.

They all sat around a table upstairs in the empty pub with a drink each. Raven was filled in on the group and

Bow brought everyone up to speed with Raven's meeting with Brother Oxford.

"Pretty cool. So you reckon together you can give us some extra asset?" Ash asked.

"It will take time, but Bow's a powerful witch, and I apparently have all this strength, so yeah," Raven answered.

"But it has to be something that's already in you, if that makes sense," Bow added.

"So I guess our wings? I had them once and the angel blood still runs through Ash and my veins," Zen enquired.

"Yes, but maybe we could work it out so they're not permanent, maybe on demand," Raven suggested to Bow.

"Absolutely, so River, there's loads of possibilities – perhaps you will be able to anticipate any attacks faster or something?" Bow thought.

"That'd be cool. I think you two just literally being together has made us stronger, I can feel it," River replied.

"So what will you do with me?" Punk asked.

"You're super clever already, but I think you could do with a little confidence!" Bow observed.

Punk smiled gratefully.

"In the mean time guys, I think I have a distraction," Raven admitted.

Bow looked at him, proud and infatuated.

"Spill Bruv," Ash said.

"Word on the street is there's a tour guide on Broad Street getting a lot of attention of late but I had a dream about him, I think we need to see what his deal is," Raven explained.

"Awesome, let's go," Zen shouted.

"Let's finish our drinks first," River suggested.

They all toasted to the new strength of Oxford's group of growing protectors; and to her and him: Bow and Raven.

Guide

"Roll up, roll up, you have a choice ladies and gentleman. Buy one of many local magazines and guide books; several pages of mind boggling rubbish and two free staples. Or for a small price, you can put your trust in my knowledge of the history and forbidden secrets of this fine city. If I were to say I was a psychic, I would be lying. Although, dare I say it, I have friends from many eras past who have offered me their versions of events to pass on to you, good folk," said the charismatic tour guide.

'What a jerk', Ange thought to herself, although she did find him amusing. Maybe this guy would prove to be an inspiration. She stared at him in thought. He was average height, is hair was fluffy and brown. He looked about her age, late twenties to early thirties. He had rosy cheeks and a cheery glow in his eyes. His fashion sense was a little perculiar. It was hard to tell if he was wearing period costume or just a jumble of clothes he'd thrown on from a charity shop. He had on a green patterned waistcoat and coarse beige trousers. His shirt too was odd. It reminded Ange of an eighteenth century shirt with its frilly collar and full, gathered sleeves.

He saw her hesitating and said, "Don't consider for a moment longer, Miss." Being put on the spot didn't worry her, she would quite happily have thrown some abuse at him. His crafty wink though, that made her heart stop a beat. He was now right in front of her, in a blink he'd moved from the corner of Turl Street (much to the satisfaction of the hole-in-shoe *Big Issue* vendor also trying to earn a living).

"How did you know I was a 'Miss', Sir?" Ange fired sarcastically.

He smiled confidently, taking her hand daintily he whispered, "Though you strike me somewhat untraditional, most in wedlock display a ring, do they not?" He pursed his lips, pouting a kiss at her. "That will be one Great British pound, thrice, if you please?" he finished, slightly louder.

She reached in her jeans pocket heavily shoving the three quid in his palm. One way or another he was going to drive her crazy.

"Now then, anyone else care to join this charming young lady or do I have the pleasure of her all to myself?" he shouted to the crowd.

He had the attention of most passersby in Broad Street and at least half of them were lining up to pay him for his performance.

'This had better be good,' Ange thought.

Little did she know that it would change her life.

* * *

"Ladies and Gentleman it has been an absolute pleasure to be in your company for the past hour and a half. I dearly hope you have either learnt something or at very least enjoyed admiring the wonderful sights of Oxford. Let me finish our tour by directing your attention to a good friend of mine, Oxford's finest and only Victorian Undertaker, Mr Bill Spectre. You will find him waiting at the castle most Friday and Saturday evenings. He will not just lead you further into the darkness of Oxford but also to meet the very ghosts that walk these streets and, I believe, even the devil! Do yourselves a favour, Ladies and Gentleman, take yourselves to the castle and experience the most enjoyable couple of hours you could have in this city. And on that note, I bid you good day!" said the guide. And with that he threw a smoke bomb at the pavement just a few centimetres from his feet and vanished in front of the crowd of people standing around him on Bonn Square.

The crowd erupted in a burst of applause causing passersby to wonder what they had missed.

"Thank you, thank you very much indeed!" he said as he appeared again bowing behind the crowd he had two seconds ago been facing.

"Sir, that was most impressive! What a splendid tour," said a man from the crowd, and held out his hand for the tour guide to shake.

"Why, thank you," the guide obliged.

Many more complimented him on his tour but he had his mind on the young lady who had caught his eye earlier.

The guide shook hands and thanked all those from the tour that approached him. Finally, as the crowd dispersed, the red haired girl who had been waiting all the while, approached him.

"So how did you do it?" she quizzed him.

"Now then, why would I tell a pretty young journalist such?" he replied confidently.

"So it seems you're a psychic as well as an illusionist?"

"Now now, if you had been listening you'd remember I claimed not to be a psychic at the start of the tour. Luck has it I have a few connections here and there who let me know who is who. But even so, you gave yourself away with the discreet notes you scribbled down."

"Not so discreet, then. Educational - of course."

"Well, yes if you wanted to educate yourself about me," he replied. Before she could say anything he tapped the tip of his nose and then continued, "Let's just say I have friends who look over shoulders. Now if you wanted to learn about me all you needed to do was ask. Why don't I buy you a drink?" he nodded his head toward The Bell and Compass pub.

"Based on your cheek alone I would decline, but because you leave me in wonder, I fear I might accept this once."

He smiled, "Shall we forget the promise of only *one* drink and leave the rest to depend on how our meeting unfolds?"

"Very well," she replied with a hint of a smirk.

The bar had a nice atmosphere, clean, classy and cosy. They took their drinks and sat down at a table on the raised seating area.

"So, there is something about you. You have a secret," she asked, taking no time to jump in, just like he expected her to.

"Hey, slow down girl, you're on fire. You have a secret too – your name."

"Ange," she answered without hesitating.

"And my name, in case you have forgotten, is Guy. Don't we all have secrets, isn't that what life is about?"

"Aren't you just charismatic - no give? You like to be in control, and you know what? I can't decide if I like you."

"Ok, I'll give you this honey, I do have a secret but given my past I'm enjoying having a turn in the driving seat, taking control of my life. So you know what's beautiful about that? What is beautiful about that is I couldn't give a damn who doesn't like it."

Ange raised her eyebrows as she sipped her wine. She looked down at the dark wooden table thinking for a minute and then asked, "So are you local?"

"You could say that," he answered. He hadn't touched his pint, just sat back casually – cupping his palm around the glass. He pursed his lips, leant forwards and said, "You know Ange, there is so much I could tell you, incredible secrets in this city you couldn't even begin to dream of. I'll share a couple with you if you get off my back for a while."

"You've got my attention, Guy. I'll trade you your privacy for the secrets of the city," Ange said.

That was one less worry off Guy's mind, he didn't need someone looking into his past.

"Well then, I shall see you again. Let's say ten a.m. tomorrow, Bulwarks Lane. I trust you know where that is?" he said and stood up. As he did, he discreetly inspected his hands, they were losing matter and threatening to be dissolved by the rush of air that was whirling around them. Swiftly he took her hand, kissed it with as much delicacy as time would let him and then out he rushed causing the remaining clientele to turn their attention to the table which he had departed so suddenly. Left alone was Ange and a full pint of cider at his absent place.

"That was a close call, kid," said a tall elderly gentleman dressed in a long grey jacket, who stood smoking a pipe at the corner of Bulwarks Lane.

"Tell me about it," Guy agreed.

"You know you're special, but whatever your gift, it looks like it's running out," the gentleman added.

They both stood watching the city go about its daily life, both invisible to everyone in it.

Guy stood in the very same spot much longer than the sympathetic spectre who had now wandered off. He stood alone, staring at the starry sky, still invisible to the city. He was surrounded by thousands of people walking by - but he had never felt more alone. Not only had his body faded, but with it had dissolved his high level of energy.

Before he had died he'd been a writer, but no-one had noticed him in the city. They didn't know who he was, didn't have the slightest clue that he was the author of work that was famously loved. Even friends and family had found themselves too busy to acknowledge his hints at his loneliness. And then, the hypocrites, they had mourned and cried over his death, claiming that life would never be the same without him and how wonderful he had been.

It was as if someone or something had whispered to him that afternoon that he had taken his life. He had never been able to make sense of it to this day; the feeling that it was right, that things would be fine, as if angels were guiding him. He'd left the ale house a little drunker than usual. As he did, a hooded figure handed him one last drink. He knew it had been poisoned but nevertheless he drank it willingly. For years he would wander the city watching how it changed until recent years when he began to realise people were seeing him. He was becoming corporeal. And so he began his tours with the knowledge he had gathered from listening to all the tales of the ghosts of Oxford. The attention he was getting disguised the deep sadness he had carried around with his spirit - the sadness of his loneliness.

Then as he reached the height of his fame the curse became apparent to him, as apparent as that historic feeling that his last drink was sure to finish him. He realised his ability to choose when he was seen was slipping from his grasp. His physical form had a curfew.

"After your sharp exit yesterday I thought you weren't going to be here," a voice disturbed him from his silent musings. If the voice hadn't startled him, the bells alerting the city it was ten a.m. would have done.

"Ange," he realised, a little confused by how he'd lost so much time so quickly.

"Coffee?" she asked, with a little concern and less sarcasm to her tone this morning. "You know, anyone would think you'd been here all night."

"Heh," he attempted a laugh. He straightened up from where he had been leaning.

Over coffee he began to loosen up. They had more than one coffee and really began to click. If Ange had had her guard up initially, she had definitely dropped it now. It was like she was almost a different person, laughing at Guy's jokes, chatting like she was infatuated with him. Guy was happy. He even forgot that he needed to be worried about his secret. He willingly told Ange all the secrets of the city.

"Some are just stories; others have been sworn to me to be true. There are many cryptic messages hidden in the least expected places: in the basements of buildings, behind secret doors. Apparently there are many rituals that could put the city in grave danger."

"Ooh, do tell me more Guy," Ange persuaded. Guy was blinded by his attraction and failed to see the falseness behind her fairly good front.

"Well the most guarded secret, one I don't even mention on my tours, is the 'curse of time'. It is said that if four particular swords are found and placed in four particular towers at a particular date and time then the barriers of time itself could fall. It would cause ultimate chaos."

"Blimey, imagine it," Ange said looking enchanted. "So if one was inclined Guy, how would the details be acquired."

"Now Ange, why would anyone wish to cause such chaos? Besides I don't know the particulars, like I said it is a heavily guarded secret," Guy lied, conscious of Ange's interest.

"So what else do you have to tell me?" Ange laughed off the embarrassment of her query being rejected.

"Well, as so it happens, I'm due to start a tour at 11am, and maybe I could slip in a few stories that have been unheard of before now. Would you join me? I won't charge you this time," Guy said and smiled.

"OK, just this once then. Besides, I'm dying to get out of here for a cigarette," Ange agreed.

* * *

Guy stood on the corner of Broad Street and Turl Street.

"Ladies and Gentleman, you must stop what you are doing immediately. I can take you on an adventure around the city, through alleyways, before spectacular buildings and to the deepest darkest alleys. Furthermore, I can lead you through the paths in which the haunted wander and past the points of inspiration of many writers. Then if you have still not had enough of me in a couple of hours, I will take you to one of the city's finest taverns where you may, if you wish, buy me a drink!" boomed Guy.

As usual the crowds were gathering fast, intrigued at what the guide was offering to show them.

"Ladies and Gentleman," he continued, "we have a guest of honour joining us today, the new journalist on the block, Miss Ange. She has kindly offered to collect for me, my fee of only three British pounds." As many people lined up to pay for a place on the tour Guy turned his attention to the Big Issue vendor who was sat against the wall of Blackwell's. He was a regular in the city, struggling to make a living, long brown hair and beard, tatty, holey clothes. His business was being inched out by the newer vendors who had better sob stories ready to trot out to the gullible customers. Guy leant down and stroked the fawn short-haired old dog.

"Hey boy, are you being good for your Papa?" Guy said as he patted the dog. He quietly turned his attention to the vendor. "We'll be out of your hair in a minute mate, I feel bad when you guys are here, you know, you genuine folk. Listen, take this, I hope it will help for today," Guy said and discreetly pulled out two twenties from the inside of his waistcoat and handed it over to him. "Oh and give my best to the boys, how's old Spud?"

"Oh you know, same old Spud. Hey thanks for this chap," the vendor replied in a Northern accent.

Nodding his head and with a wink, Guy patted him on the shoulder, "Anytime fellow."

"Oh by the way, some old boy with a pipe gave me this for you, said you'd understand."

Guy took the note held out to him. Unfolding it he quickly glanced at the words:

'You need to be at Roger Bacon Lane, this afternoon. Seek out a witch who can help you with your recent problem.'

As Guy stood up he felt Ange's eyes on him between taking the money.

"Let's get going then folks!" Guy boomed in a cheerful tone.

The day ended as it had yesterday – in the pub, although this time Guy had his timing perfect. He was able to enjoy a drink and plan his exit with a little less urgency.

"Ange, it's been so wonderful spending the day with you. But, I regret I must leave now."

"Anyone would think you're seeing someone else," Ange teased.

"Well perhaps it is true that I have an appointment with another, however not for romance," Guy debated whether to tell Ange more but something stopped him. "Perhaps you would care to meet me again?"

"There's something odd about you Guy, but yeah I'd like to meet again."

"Good," Guy replied. He slowly raised himself from his chair, bowed his head slightly and confidently walked out of the bar.

He deliberately failed to repeat yesterday's kiss on

Ange's hand. He was a little unsure of her interest in him. The absence of his affection would either drive her crazy, ensuring she would return if she indeed did have feelings for him. Or if it was solely information she sought then she would realise that he would not offer further assistance.

Guy walked past the Westgate shopping centre and headed toward St Ebbes. He took a right turn past the gym and strolled to the opening of Roger Bacon Lane. A provocatively dressed girl stood a little way up the slope. Her hair was so blonde it was almost white.

"Now then, you know a girl of your age looking like that, stood in a back alley is sure to run into trouble – unless of course you're capable of looking after yourself. And if so, you must be the witch I am looking for," Guy deduced.

"Clever chap," the girl said sweetly.

"I've been told you can help me out. I've been having some problems managing my manifestation. It's only of late that this has been happening, I've lived for decades with this gift. I can't make sense of why it's fading now."

"So we have a poorly ghost? Well now, that won't do. I can help you, but it will cost you. £100 a potion, the potion will last a week a time and you will retain your 'gift'."

"No problem, I make more than that in a day. But tell me, why is this happening?"

"Sugar, you're a ghost. I don't know why you were able to be human at your will in the first place. I suppose nothing lasts forever, perhaps you have displeased the Gods, or failed to find your purpose, who knows? Anyway I've got a lot to do. I'm going to be busy for a couple of weeks, so how about you take two potions from me?"

Guy wasn't sure whether the witch was reliable but he had no choice. He gave her enough cash for two week's worth of potions. She handed him two black apothecary bottles. Then, in earnest, he grabbed her arm, "Hang on, why are you carrying these? How could you have possibly known I would come to you?"

"I'm a witch remember, there's not a lot I don't know. Now run along. Oh, and my name is Vestra, you'll find me here in two weeks time – unless the world ends of course," she cackled a bitter laugh and vanished in a cloud of smoke.

Guy was left with the sensation of tingling in his fingers, a bitter breeze surrounded his bare skin and he knew he had seconds to drink the potions before they smashed on the ground as his clasp lost matter.

He popped the corks from the bottles and chugged them both desperately. The potion made him retch, but he kept it down. He could detect the bitterness of mugwort, then the sweetness of deadly nightshade berries, and finally amongst other things the acidity of mandrake.

"Huh, some of the herbs of Samhain, makes sense I guess," Guy thought aloud.

He shook his head. The draught that was trying to consume him a couple of minutes ago had now disintegrated, he could feel human warmth in his hands running to the edge of his fingertips. Guy smiled, he was in control again. He could afford to be as arrogant as he liked.

"I knew there was something about you," a voice startled him as he clasped the empty bottles.

He turned around to see Ange stood behind him. Sternly the words fell from his lips, "How long have you been there?"

"A couple of moments after you. No wonder you know so much! Are you kidding me? You're dead? How twisted is that?" Ange screamed at him.

"Look would you keep your voice down," Guy returned. "Why don't we go somewhere and talk this out."

"Thanks Guy, but I think we've done enough talking. Go back to wherever it is you've come from," Ange stormed off. Guy couldn't see the huge grin she wore, an easy excuse to dump him having acquired what she had wanted; his knowledge.

"Ange, come back," he shouted but as much as he wanted to follow shock had paralysed his legs, like the bones had become absent, he fell to his knees smashing the bottles on the path like a drunk. Faint, he let himself go, let the human matter he had just paid so much for fade. He became invisible amongst the mosaic of broken glass. Rising hopelessly he walked. He walked for a long time. Finally he reached University Museum and retired to the loft with the bats for a couple of weeks; oblivious to the zombie crisis consuming the city caused by the witch whom he had purchased a fragment of humanity from.

* * *

The evening was upon the city. Zen and Ash casually walked to the lamppost on the corner of Turl Street where Raven had suspected the guide could be found.

"Not that I'd expect this guy to be doing tours all day and all night but it's kind of weird for someone so popular to have vanished. Don't you think babe?" Ash looked down at Zen.

"What do you mean? You think something's happened?" Zen replied. "Argh! It's so hard to think, I'm thirsty for blood. Can't we go and find some scum to feed on and then come back to this."

Ash's eyes lit up in agreement, though his expression soon dropped and he clutched his hand to Zen's shoulder.

"Not on my watch, thank you," said River and dropped to the floor from the lamp. "I can't believe you two were actually going to head off for blood when you're supposed to be on a sacred mission. One of our brothers is lost."

"Actually, we think we might know where he is. We put our heads together and..." Bow called approaching hand in hand with Raven.

"Spare me the details. Where do you think he is?" River cut in.

"I was going to say we think he's at the museum," Bow finished.

"How do you do that?" Punk interrupted appearing from the Magdalen Street way.

"Well, now Raven and I have bonded it's just a case of deep meditation and focus. A joint vision led us to the museum, but we don't know which part. There's still ground to explore once we get there," Bow finished.

"Cool, so more breaking in?" Ash interjected.

"Come on, guys, just because our vision led us to the museum, it doesn't mean he is going to stay, if in fact we are on the right lines at all," Raven pointed out in the hope of regaining the group's focus.

The six of them walked as quickly as possible, a little nervous at discovering a potentially new member of their group. Hand in hand Zen and Ash walked behind Raven and Bow. Punk and River followed behind casually chatting, so intent on their friendship that neither of them could spot the other's affection.

Soon they were standing before a grand building. Casts of dinosaur feet were filling with rain water on the grass where they paused.

"The museum's alarms are going to be too strong to allow us to get in," Bow said.

"So you're saying that technology overpowers magick?" Punk asked.

"No, I'm saying physical beings are enough to trigger beams," Bow replied.

"Fair point, but your magick is ridiculously strong, surely there's a way of counteracting them or making us somehow invisible to the beams," Punk wondered.

"My magick may be strong but I wouldn't want to test it when we don't know for sure that we're right. We could cause all sorts of trouble," Bow argued.

"She's right Punk, it's not worth it," River added gently. "Besides, have you ever been in that place with the thunder and lightning above, jeeesh, always makes me think the exhibits are coming to life."

"What's on your mind Ash?" Raven enquired as he noticed Ash whisper to Zen.

Ash and Zen sprinted leaping on to the wall of the magnificent structure. "Bats!" Ash shouted back. The vampires scurried up the side of the museum to the roof.

Turning to look at the group from the great height Zen elaborated, "With CCTV operating in the building what are the chances a guy is going to be hanging around the floor. If he's in here like you suspect he'll be in the roof and so we can shout to him through the bat holes."

"The vampire's have a point you know," Punk said.

The grounded four looked up in anticipation.

Hugging the roof of the tower Ash called in, "Hey dude, Mr tour guide, if you're in there, then I think we're looking for you."

Zen raised an eyebrow. Ash shrugged his shoulders and smiled at Zen's expression.

Guy, inside the tower, sat wandering if he was dreaming vividly. Then he heard a second voice. "Well if he is in there, he doesn't want to be found," Zen said.

"WAIT!" Guy made himself jump. "You won't be able to see me."

"We've found him," Ash called down.

"What do you mean?" Zen asked gently.

"I'm a ghost. It's kind of complicated," Guy replied warily.

"Trust me bruv, we're experts at 'complicated'," Ash reassured.

"You were right, I was a tour guide, I had a gift which enabled me to appear human by choice. Then for some reason the power slipped so I acquired a potion to fix it. Around the same time I met some girl, she found out my secret and, well, was pretty much disgusted. I figured I may as well just fade away so I came up here out of the way. The potion has run out anyhow, so until I acquire another one from this witch Vestra, you won't be seeing me anytime soon," Guy explained miserably.

"Vestra? Vestra's an evil bitch who's been taken down by our very own sorceress - the best and most powerful in the city to be precise," Zen said.

"Mate, I'd bet anything Vestra had cursed you in order to sell you a remedy, nothing Bow can't fix. Look the deal is you're actually pretty special. You're part of a calling, a calling chosen to protect the city for eternity. You've already sat out a zombie crisis and some other mishaps but between you and me I think there'll be plenty more strife upon us. So what do you say? Get your ghostly arse outta there and we'll fill you in," Ash spoke man to man.

Zen smiled at him admiringly.

"Ok chap. I'll make my way to the front of the museum," Guy said with a slight detection of positivity in his voice.

Hands entwined, Zen and Ash jumped into a graceful soar to the grass joining the others.

"What's the deal?" River enquired.

"Two bitches in one day sent him into a depression, one of them being Vestra, I think he's been hexed by her. So he's a ghost, but he's no ordinary ghost. Before Vestra came on the scene he was able to choose between human and spirit form, now he's stuck as a ghost, unable to manifest. He's our guy I reckon. Do you reckon you guys can help him?" Ash turned to Bow and Raven.

"Hi folks, I'm here. My name is Guy by the way," Guy said, invisible to them all.

"Hi Guy, look we can help you but you need to commit ultimate focus. This is Raven, he is a human forged by the Gods, a shrine of strength. Can you stand between us and do exactly as I say," Bow instructed.

"Ok," Guy replied, his voice now between them.

Bow and Raven held hands.

"This will be interesting. If you guys can do this then we're next for the wings I ordered," Ash joked.

"Ok, Guy, I want you to feel the rain, I want you to

feel the cold, remember what it's like to be human, remember every single detail of your life, every single pain, moment of pleasure, every insult, every compliment, everything that made you human. Raven, are you ready? Remember what he looked like in your vision, let's do this."

"I'm ready sweetheart," Raven replied.

They both closed their eyes. The rain was pouring down on them, they were drenched through but this fact did not dampen their concentration. In fact they embraced it; the water was an asset, a gift from the gods. It represented a cycle and before Punk, River, Ash and Zen's eyes a current of rainbow electricity sparked in a circuit flooding from shoulder to shoulder. The current sped faster throwing off embers of magick as it did.

"Ok, Guy, this bit is going to hurt, hold on tight," Raven shouted.

"NOOOOOOOOOOOOOO!" Guy's tortured soul screeched, then like a hologram flickering, becoming clearer the tour guide knelt in the mud and keeled over as he was reborn.

There was a huge explosion which repelled Bow and

Raven seventy miles per hour away from each other, landing at opposite ends of the museum grounds.

In either disbelief or relief – it wasn't quite apparent which – Guy slowly stood up, he inspected his hands and body intently and finally smiled a radiant grin.

He laughed, and then he jumped and then skipped to River who he gave a tremendous hug. "I'm here, and you can see me!" he said.

Bow and Raven made their way back to each other, semi-exhausted.

"You know Vestra's curses should have dispersed with her power. It was your own doubt that had sealed your invisibility," Raven explained.

"However can I thank you?" Guy wondered.

"How's about we go to church?" Bow suggested.

"Church?" Guy's voice squeaked.

"Yeah, but not to pray, to enrol you to your destiny. I've got a feeling you're gonna like the priest, dude, he's got a thing about manifestation," Punk added.

"We'll explain everything on the way. Welcome to the gang," Ash congratulated, shaking Guy's hand.

"St Giles then?" Zen wondered.

"St Giles it is," River concluded.

They all walked to the local church to initiate their new brother. Not only would Guy be welcomed by a ghost monk, but the next day by an excitable crowd of punters hoping to learn of the secrets he could share.

And as for Ange, well perhaps Guy would see her again, but not for a while anyway.

Ghouls of Grandpont

"Are you excited about the camping trip this weekend? It will be top stuff," Luke said to Trent, Lucy, Amy and Sarah as they walked out of Magdalan College towards The Plain and home.

"Sure, it will be fun. Remind me where it is again?" Amy enquired.

"There are supposedly some haunted farm fields between Grandpont Nature Reserve and one of the cricket grounds behind Hinskey Park – if you didn't know where they were you wouldn't ever find them," Luke revealed.

"Luckily for us my brother told me how to get to them. There's so much ground there to be explored, I thought we could start a campfire by 'The Fingers', it would make some pretty sweet photos," Trent proposed.

"How much trouble is this going to get us into?" Amy wondered.

"You girls are too paranoid; we'll be fine, as long as we're on the farmland by the morning when the nature reserve is inspected," Luke was confident that they were going to have fun and still manage to stay at Oxford University, even if with a first disciplinal warning.

"So, haunted?" Lucy asked, sceptically.

"Yeah, there are loads of stories of spooks showing at night, although apparently the tales are told by rough sleepers. So maybe it's just a ploy to keep people away from their peaceful hideouts. Still, can't go wrong with a picnic of beers, supper over a campfire and some stories and dares right?" Trent swept his hand through his shoulder–length mousey brown hair, knowing that the girls wouldn't miss this weekend with him for the world. There would be a group of ten of them in total, the forecast was ok for the early evening but the night would be wet with thunderstorms, just what he had hoped, scared girls were easy.

"Ghosts are not real, nor are vampires or witches – shall I go on? It's just all down to the atmosphere; the brain is capable of misinterpreting shadows in moments of fear," Sarah said confidently and not falling for Trent's charms like Lucy and Amy, she and Luke were tight.

"We'll see," Trent replied miming a kiss at her.

Saturday evening soon came round and they reached Grandpont through Whitehouse Road. The rest of the group had made their way from behind the Ice Rink and met them at the campsite.

A camp fire was already burning in the middle of the huge wooden sculpture of an oversized hand that seemed to burst forth from the ground. It was an awe inspiring landmark, like a giant pushing his way up from the underworld.

"So who's ready to be spooked?" Luke asked.

"What are you waiting for?" an unfamiliar voice said from somewhere behind him. A ghostly jogger, illuminated from within, ran on the track opposite. Only Trent had noticed and heard him.

"Whatever, let's get this thing started," Trent said choosing to ignore what he had just seen. He knew very well that vampires, ghosts and witches were just a few of the actual things that did exist and were active in Oxford, though he was too cool to admit it.

"Everyone sit down, we'll start with some gentle gossip shall we?"

Ten students of the university sat crossed legged around a campfire with their bottles of alcohol, marshmallows and popcorn. Behind them was a group of spirits, currently unseen to them, but ready to have a party of their own.

Axel and Sky managed to slip away from the university gossip that had taken off instead of the ghost stories that were supposed to have begun. They were both into old school eighties rock and dressed like Emos, although despite the stereotype they were happy normal kids, not manically depressed, in fact they weren't happier than if they were having a drink and a spliff. For a while they'd been keen on each other but rather than advertise their affections publically they'd been enjoying meeting up away from their friends. Nothing had happened between them yet; although Sky was going crazy for the moment Axel made his first move and Axel loved the fact that Sky was trying to be subtle about her feelings for him. He thought tonight would be the perfect night to seduce her. They were hidden by a group of trees just behind The Fingers where the others were warming up around the fire.

"Happy birthday by the way sweetheart," Axel said to Sky, brushing her long fringe from her eye.

"Thanks, honey," Sky replied - it was the perfect day, the day of her nineteenth year, and it would be celebrated out in the star filled night.

"I got you a present by the way," Axel reached his hand into his inside jacket pocket; he looked at her admiringly, "Here," he handed her a black crystal, it had been smoothed around the edges into a sphere.

"Oh wow, sweet! Thank you!" she was impressed.

"It's not just a stone babe, the guy I bought it from on Gloucester Green Market said it apparently had some magick held in it, so close your eyes and make a wish," Axel put his arms around her.

Sky placed the gem into the pouch she wore around her neck; she closed her eyes and thought silently, 'I want tonight to be a night never to forget.'

She opened her eyes and looked at Axel, he was handsome, and sure of the music and style he loved, everything she wanted.

He moved his right arm around both of her shoulders and gently tilted her chin to meet his lips, they were in a moment, their lip piercings gently clattered as they kissed, giving them away to the rest of the group.

"Ah there you guys are, should've known you were an item, come on lovers," Jayde, their close fun loving friend joked, making them both jump.

Axel looked at Sky reassuringly before he turned to greet Jayde.

"So we are going to keep this quiet from the posers out there?" he asked quietly.

"You guys were just stretching your legs right?" Jayde winked at them both.

Sky was about to say thank you, when out of the corner of her eye she noticed a figure, she turned to look but no-one was there.

"What's up buddy?" Jayde asked Sky.

"Nothing, just my mind playing tricks, I guess it's the atmosphere. Let's join the others," she replied, on edge a little.

Once again the group were reunited, Trent with his arm around Lucy, Sarah on Luke's lap. Blake, an athletic and handsome lad was sat with Amy, who was keen on both him and Malachi. Malachi was a pale, hippy type, who wore his dreads behind a bandana but was more interested in his books than girls. And finally Jayde, Sky and Axel had sat down to complete the circle.

Blake passed Sky and Axel a beer each, as they settled in.

"So, I'll start. Did you know there's a rumour that one woman was horrifically killed here over a drugs dispute and her ghost can be seen playing hide and seek around the fields?" Trent said, showing off.

"Shall we go and find her?" Jayde suggested, knowing Trent was really a wimp behind his facade.

"How was she killed?" Lucy asked, trying to attract Trent's attention.

"Stabbed to death apparently, some people think she wears a red blouse but actually it is the blood from her wounds," Trent continued.

"Oh my god! There she is!" Luke screamed sincerely.

Everyone shouted - some covered their eyes; Trent leapt up to peg it.

Luke was in hysterics, "Oh come on, really? It was a joke. You ran like a girl Trent."

"I was playing along dude," Trent lied.

Luke received a few hard slaps on the arm from the girls. They moaned as their hearts still raced from their fright in the darkness. Their relief was interrupted.

A high pitch ear-splitting scream echoed through the motion of the passing cargo train; "H e e e e e e e e e l l l l l l l l l l l l l l l l l l l p p p p p p p p p p Meeeeeeeeeeeeeeeeeeeeeeeeeeeeee!"

The lively atmosphere collapsed, the group sat frozen in fear and almost disbelief. Like mice turned to statues hiding from a predator, no-one dare moved until the train had passed and then for even a few seconds after that.

"What the ..?! What was that?" Malachi was the first to speak.

"It was probably just the wheels on the train," Axel suggested rationally.

"No, no, it sounded like someone just jumped under the fricking train!" Amy said with shock over her face.

"I had a weird feeling earlier but didn't want to say, I thought I saw someone out of the corner of my eye," Sky admitted.

"You're not the only one; I thought we were being watched too," Blake admitted.

"Ok, maybe we should move on, we've obviously had the effect we were after here, didn't you say we could pitch up our tent in some farm fields?" Sarah asked Trent.

"Yeah, we'll move on," Trent said happily.

"We'll leave the fire burning, in case we need to head back – it will burn out itself eventually," Luke said.

"Ok, let's pack up, even if it is our imagination I think we're gonna end up freaking out here, at least the fields will be more open," Jayde suggested.

They all grabbed something to carry and made their way through paths covered by arches made from the bowing branches of the huge trees. The rain fell as the forecast had promised; thunder put them on edge and the lightening lit up the path. The group continued to reassure each other that the figures they were seeing were just a mixture of their intoxicated brains and the flashes of lightening. They eventually reached the opening overlooking the river under the train bridge.

"Any of your ghost friends here mate?" Blake asked Trent.

"Well a few overdoses and I think someone drowned here but let's just keep walking. The fields are just past the bridge, just remember if a train comes over it will sound like the bridge is collapsing above you so move fast," Trent warned beginning to think that this trip was a bad idea. Come to think of it, his brother had never been the same since he'd returned that summer from university.

Past the green rickety graffiti-ridden train bridge Luke shone a torch at a discreet path to the left leading to a stile, just before the little white wooden railed bridge that crossed the river. One by one they avoided the muddy puddle and headed into the acres of empty farmland for what they thought might be a more relaxed evening. Unbeknown to them, their night of hell was just beginning.

Sky took her turn to climb the stile. Being the last she was nervous and desperate to reach the side of the fence where her friends waited. A gust of wind thrust a nearby branch in her face. As the branch bounced back it caught her necklace pouch, the drawstring loosened and out fell the stone that Axel had earlier given to her. It rolled down a nearby rabbit hole never to be seen again and sure to keep Grandpont active with the power of its magick.

Oblivious of losing the stone, in her fear she leapt down nearly slipping on the damp rotting wood of the stile. She fell into Axel's arms. The rest of the group had headed for a clearing between lines of trees to set up the huge tent they had packed.

"Come on, hopefully they've got it pitched by now – eight pitching a tent shouldn't take long right?" Axel reassured Sky trying to disguise the nervousness in his voice, he felt like he was being watched from every direction.

"Oh my, what the...?" Sky screamed.

Tearing across the first field was a huge black panther, paws pounding and throat growling. Even if they were in disbelief at what they were seeing they took no time to wonder before they ran for their lives.

"IS THAT TENT UP YET?" Axel bellowed as he and Sky reached the clearing.

Amazingly the big blue gazebo of a tent was, and although it would not offer much protection from a wild cat it was better than nothing.

Running like they had never run before Axel and Sky skidded into the fabric porch, with no hesitation they zipped up the door. A look of horror painted across their faces.

"What the hell were you running from?" Blake quizzed.

"I am not lying, there is a...a...full size...black...panther...out...outside!" Axel explained between breaths.

"Dude, if there was panther chasing you it would have ripped this tent to shreds by now and all of us," Malachi offered.

"I'll check it out," Jayde said confidently.

"Are you crazy?" Sky knew it seemed impossible but she knew what they had seen and didn't want to lose a friend.

"Chuck me the torch will you Luke," Jayde said ignoring her friend's concern. She caught the light easily – Luke was an accurate throw. Unzipping the tent fearlessly she wandered out. The torch brightly lit up the area. There was nothing in sight and certainly no big cat growling. To make sure she did a quick sweep around the large tent.

"What?!" Jayde burst out. She drew out her phone and took a photo of a large cat-like impression in the long grass. It was deep enough to suggest that whatever had made it had lain there for some time. As she closed the camera app on her phone she noticed the time was wrong. "What the hell is going on?" she questioned under her breath, returning to the tent.

"Guys, what time do you make it?" she asked.

"Just after... hang on a minute, two in the morning? How can that be?" Sarah was confused.

"We've lost time, I don't know how, it's impossible, but it seems that hours have dissolved in minutes," Jayde said. "And check this out, Axel and Sky weren't joking," she showed her friends the photo. They crowded around the phone.

"I don't like it here guys, I think we should get out here and go home," Lucy declared.

"Yeah, but to leave here we have to get through this field and through Grandpont, otherwise it's a long walk around Botley to get back into town. I think we should just sit tight and leave as soon as it is light," Trent suggested.

Blake was just about to recommend a vote in favour, his voice however crumbled. Everyone sat petrified just as they had when the eerie train had passed earlier. A tediously slow squeaking silenced them, next a vision that they all witnessed: a small hay cart travelling through the very spot where they sat. There was no vision of the peasant who was damned to eternally pull it, just the haunting image accompanied with an atrociously frightening squeal. It seemed to take forever but it did eventually cease and the ten students came out of their trance-like state.

"Let's just sit tight, huddle up if necessary," Blake was the first to speak.

"Get as much drink down your necks as you can, hopefully we'll just pass out," Amy said handing out alcohol.

"Not a bad idea," Sarah agreed dragging the bag of booze to the centre of the tight semi-circle.

The students were terrified, and as quickly as possible guzzled plenty of alcohol. Soon they were all asleep but they had been foolish to think they would be at peace whilst they rested.

* * *

Two men dressed in nineteen thirties attire dragged another man by his elbows across fields from North

Hinskey Village. His wrists were cuffed with knotted fabric and his mouth gagged.

They placed a tired wooden chair that had been carried by one of the men near the edge of the water. Carelessly they threw their prisoner onto it. The shorter fairer haired man rolled up his sleeves; from inside his waistcoat he pulled a pistol.

"You have one chance, tell us where it is or you're dead. Do you understand me? Dead."

The taller well-built man lowered the gag. Tears escaped from the victim's eyes as he blurted out in a sob, "I've told you, I don't know."

With no hesitation the armed gangster shot his firearm. The rickety chair collapsed as the bullet struck the man and as it did it fell into the stream taking the body with it.

"Make sure this is cleaned up," the murderer instructed, walking away.

* * *

Trent noticed Malachi was waking up, "Hey mate, I'm glad you're up, I just heard the freakiest thing. Some guy just got shot."

"No way, I just dreamt that," Malachi said sleepily.

The rest of the group woke at the sound of their voices.

"What's this?" Jayde quizzed.

"A murder that he dreamt, I heard," Trent filled in.

"'You have one chance, tell us where it is or you're dead, do you understand me? Dead,'" Sky said robotically.

Shivers scuttled down every single person's spine as they realised they had all in one way or another witnessed the same incident. Leaving no time for further discussion and with no rational reason, the tent caught alight.

"GET OUT OF HERE, GET OUT!" Amy screamed.

It was morning, silently the students made their way out of the fields. As they reached Whitehouse Road they parted without a word. Not one of the ten of them would ever be the same again.

* * *

"So, I heard Grandpont is full of stuff going on," Punk said that same afternoon in his apartment with his new close friends.

"Grandpont, chap, are you kidding me – even I don't go there if I can help it," Guy concluded.

"Well – if a ghost is scared then that pretty much sums it up, right?" River laughed.

"Yeah, think we're good. Hey, pass us another can mate," Ash asked cheerfully.

"You lazy git," Zen teased.

"I'll get it," Raven offered with an empty glass of his own.

"What a sweetie," Bow boasted.

Oxford's protectors enjoyed a relaxed afternoon of casual chat and drink in a brief lull of the misadventures that the troupe had met with so far.

Demon Decoy Transport Trauma

The busy roads of Oxford were often a cause of tension in the rush hour. Commuters on edge, noise escalating; the city's large population was always apparent during these times. The care-free in this messy pollution were the drivers of the two most used bus companies. Some cheerful, others grumpy but either way care-free for the traffic, as their duty was simply to drive the diverse passengers to and from their destinations. Being demons also played a factor in their carelessness, besides demons had no particular place to go during the day. Occasionally the bus companies would recruit humans. The demons couldn't look too suspicious even if they did do a marvellous job in their own human disguises. The human employees were fairly easy to spot however – way too talkative, some would even whistle. As much as the passengers annoyed the demon drivers, they had made a pact with the slayer, who you should also know, they very much disliked. The slayer though was fair, the demons were doing a job and had made a pact that they would not harm any human, she was even allocated an eternal bus pass; in return she would not destroy them. The fall in the pact for the slayer however was the demon's compensation, every Samhain night, or All Hallows Eve as you might know it, the demons were allowed a night off from their promise, but so was the slayer. It was a cat and mouse affair for the slayer to keep the commuters of Oxford from harm between the hours of six pm and midnight each thirty-first of October. Tonight, as you may have guessed, was the thirty-first of October.

This year however the slayer had an advantage, a team of warriors at her side initiated into a sacredly selected group, informally known as Oxford's protectors to the few who actually knew of their existence. Aside from the slayer, they were two vampiric angels, a watcher, a very powerful witch, a human power source forged by the Gods, and a recently recruited ghost tour guide.

Carfax clock tower struck six pm.

Seven beings sworn to protect their much loved city stood overlooking the crossroads from the tower.

"Bow, do you reckon you can manage to paralyse the buses from here, cause some fault or something, but no casualties?" River asked.

The young witch who hadn't used to be fond of heights looked at the buses emerging; she took a deep breath for focus, "I shall try Riv'," she replied to her dear slayer friend.

"I think Raven should stick with Bow, if those conniving goblin looking demons learn that Raven is the key to our strength then we don't just risk losing power but one of the group," Punk suggested. He was the logical of the group, and was River's oldest friend and watcher.

"Good plan, how fit are you feeling?" River asked him.

"I'll fight by your side," he answered tensing his huge arm muscles.

"Ash, Zen?" River asked the vampiric angel couple.

"We'll take Castle Street and Queen's, if you guys can cover The High and St Aldates? They can only hurt humans in the city centre right?"

"Yes, that's what I overheard, must be some curse on them that we don't know of," Guy, the dead tour guide of Oxford offered.

"Fine, that sounds good, Guy. What can you do?" Zen wondered.

"I'll round up a few of the spirits who have nothing better to do, we can cause distractions," Guy replied. He then dematerialised.

"Six hours, that is all. We've had to fight for days at a time in the past, we can do this. Remember no killing unless they hurt any humans, don't let them fool you either, make sure they show their true faces before you strike. Good luck," said River and edged toward the turrets of the old church's tower to join Zen and Ash who had simply been leaning over from the external side.

"Uh, no way," Punk commented.

"Come on Bruv, it's not like we're going to let you drop is it," Ash said as Punk backed away from the rope-less abseil to the ground.

"Whimp," River chucked him her bunch of skeleton keys so he could exit through the public entrance.

Bow visualised the view she had just memorised from behind closed eyes, in her imagination she halted the buses. Raven stood by her side. "If you see any demon attacks we'll go for fire action," she said.

Ash and Zen headed to their side of the bus routes whilst River waited for Punk to reach the ground, safely.

As Punk made his way out of the porch River approached him with an idea, "Looks like Bow has the buses under control but we haven't got them all, if we can somehow inform the passengers that the services are off tonight we may be able to get them to take different transport home, what do you think?"

Before Punk was able to answer Zen and Ash appeared before them. "Yeah, we have a dilemma," Zen said.

"They've somehow opened a porthole; all the buses are going through it - full of passengers," Ash continued delicately.

"That's not all kids, I've just heard that it's some sort of alternate reality of Oxford city centre, they're planning a party – human hide and seek, oh yeah and then they feast," Guy appeared before them.

"Damn it!" River shouted.

"What is it?" Bow shouted from Carfax.

"We're going on holiday," Punk shouted back up.

"Demon decoy, looks like we're going on a dimension diversion. Lovely," River said under her breath very frustrated.

Bow looked at Raven, "I was hoping to have a lush Samhain night at home together when this was all done, not risk our lives in a completely different dimension."

"When this is over we'll make up for time, I promise, I know it's annoying but if it wasn't for this sort of thing then we probably wouldn't even be together," he reassured her, delicately brushing her long fringe from her face and looking at her with his special gaze. "Follow me," he said.

She did to the dark staircase of the tower whilst everyone on the street was trying to devise a plan and calm down River. He stopped just a little way down, a step lower than Bow. Leaning into the wall of the tower he held her near to him, their lips met and she was reminded that no matter what the circumstances, being with him was all that mattered.

"How do you want to go about this?" he asked her.

"I'm assuming you mean once we're in crazy land? We need to think like people, where do people run? We need to somehow guide people into one place and merge the two realities, and preferably keep the demons locked in. I can't do that all by myself," Bow said.

"You won't need to - we'll be doing it together," Raven reminded her.

"Wait, I just realised, there's no guarantee our magick will work in that dimension," Bow thought.

"Ok, well let's go and speak to the others, see if they can manage fighting off the demons and guiding people to safe places so that we can work from this reality."

Soon Bow and Raven were inside the Radcliffe Camera – the heart of Oxford's magick source, spells had cloaked the space they had chosen and hid them from the building's security. They sat cross legged on the cross section of a large T shaped table. Candles lit around them as Bow spoke the words to communicate with the Higher Powers. They held hands and slipped into a form of meditation. They were able to communicate with one another, even to the group who were finding their way into the alternate reality dimension of the city centre. The horrific aerial view of the demon set up was visible to Bow and Raven. Torches of bare fire were lit at various points and the buses were parked up at Gloucester Green which seemed to be the only extension of the circle trap which covered the usual area between the north, east, south and west gate markers. People were screaming, running into the false city, trying to get into shops that were just illusions. The only material buildings were the historical ones but the three that Bow and Raven were hoping to use as havens were the Radcliffe Camera, Sheldonian Theatre and Town Hall.

The demon's city centre was black from the blanket of smoke concealing it. Flickers of angry red and orange flames disturbed the darkness lighting semi-familiar ground to the screaming humans who were scurrying around like frightened rodents. Guy had earlier discovered that the entrance to the demon dimension was in Friars Entry. As always the team had pulled through. Bow and Raven were ready to try and merge the dimensions, Guy, stayed in the real city centre guarding the gateway whilst Punk, River, Zen and Ash charged through the door of the 'Free House' – 'Far from the Madding Crowd'. The other side of the pub's door did not lead them to the bar but at the demon dimension crossroads of George Street where hell itself seemed to greet them.

"It seems the Higher Powers are smiling upon us once again," Ash said and leant down to pick up a mace.

"Sweet!" Punk shouted, lifting a morning-star club.

"Watch where you swing those things – I don't want to be staked by accident!" Zen snapped at the boys who were acting like first school kids.

Punk bounced the smooth part of the spiked club up and down in his palm smiling, whilst Ash put his mace by his side.

River and Zen leant down to pick up their medieval spiked weapons which handily lay at their feet.

"Remember only if you see their true identity, no human casualties," River ordered as they stuck together, marching maliciously toward Broad Street.

Like glowing beacons they stood out, their rebellious march soon became a demon frenzy as they were charged at by now unmasked, scale faced, red eyed creatures. Each demon was different, like humans they all had their own features and characteristics. But like humans they also were fragile if you knew how to destroy them.

Punk slipped away running towards Market Street then onto Cornmarket to make his way, hopefully quicker and quieter, than the others, to Turl Street, and then to the Sheldonian, collecting victims on the way and leading them to safety.

There were the odd demons patrolling the back streets, but none that Punk couldn't take care of. He had quite a gathering of people by the time he reached the Sheldonian.

Bow and Raven mentally witnessed the troubles their friends were having. Bow tried and tried to merge the two dimensions; even with Raven's power it was impossible. The two visualisations would not link as Bow had originally thought they would – instead they repelled.

Bow spoke aloud to all of her friends as if being projected by a megaphone only accessible to their ears, their own tech free conference call, "Guys, I can't merge the dimensions. I'm sorry but one way or another it's death."

"Can you not lead the humans back through the porthole?" Guy wondered.

"It's useless, there is no door way this side," Zen replied.

"We've got to destroy the demons, if they are weakened then perhaps their magick will be!" Ash added.

River hesitated, she was going to argue, try and make this a peaceful end. Mentally quarrelling with herself she tried to decide if forgiveness could be had after what the demons had done tonight. Deafening screams of humans being disembowelled pierced the atmosphere. The sight of innocent commuters being eaten violently sent rage through her. "They need to be obliterated," she said through gritted teeth.

"We'll never take them all down. We need to know their weakness," Ash advised.

"Punk, how do we destroy them?" Zen said.

"Water! Of course, why didn't I remember earlier? Once claimed by water they're bound, prisoners to it, in fact they can't breathe without it – they evolve," Punk remembered.

"So that's why the buses won't go down Abingdon Road when it floods, if the bus becomes stuck they face having to come into contact with the rain," Guy said from the real city centre, listening in.

"Riv', I can't use my magick, it's hopeless in their dimension," Bow admitted.

"No, but you and Raven have contact with them upstairs, I suggest you start praying to Poseidon, and Guy, take a visit to Brother Oxford – order a tsunami," said River.

"Friends, once the demons are wet there should be a window for Bow and Raven to merge the dimensions – even if temporarily. The hostages will be saved and set free, perhaps a little confused but still – free," Guy offered.

"Let's do it,"Ash said.

The demons were strong and coming at Ash, Zen and River fast. The weapons were helping but they were seriously outnumbered.

Punk was leading many weeping frightened people into the Sheldonian. Unfortunately there weren't as many survivors as he'd hoped and so the need to fill the Radcliffe Camera and Town Hall was no longer.

"Come on, hurry! Make your way into the theatre, try and remain calm. I'm going to hold the doors," said Punk.

Once everyone was safely inside Punk unbuckled his belt and attached it around the inner handles of the exterior doors, hoping they would resist the ravenous demons.

He ran up over one hundred steps to the tower of the Sheldonian, trying to catch sight of his friends.

"BROTHER OXFORD!" Guy ran through the wood and glass doors into St Mary Magdalan Church.

Brother Oxford stood looking down on the church with just his bony hands exposed under his long robe on the rim of the pulpit, his face as usual hardly existent under his hood.

"We need your help sir, before it's too late; we need the Higher Powers to create a tsunami in the demon decoy dimension," Guy explained.

"Surely with the strength of the group a water pipe could be burst by smashing through the roads with the weapons?" queried Brother Oxford.

"Sir, it seems there are illusions everywhere, everyone has tried their best but with all due respect sir, we need some extra help."

"Very well Guy, I shall have a word. Warn your friends they may need to fly," said Brother Oxford.

"Thank you sir, I shall," Guy bowed his head, and then sprinted from the church, knowing everyone would have heard the conversation. He simply made his way back to Friars Entry as fast as he could – in case there were any stowaway demons.

"River, it's coming, we can see the water, you guys need to get to higher ground whilst Raven and I try and merge the dimensions once more," Bow warned.

"You ready?" Raven asked Bow.

"We've got to go, come on Riv, time to test these new wings Raven gave us," Ash said.

Like subconsciously moving a limb, Ash and Zen opened their wings, their wings which would grow on demand. They were huge and so strong they knocked at least ten demons to the ground as they grew - larger than Zen's had been during the short time she was an angel, however still the same elegant shade of black. River - not quite knowing what putting her life literally in friend's hands would be like – held onto both Zen and Ash's hands as they all sprinted. They took off.

"WHOOHOO!" River shouted. Flying freely was not just amazing in itself but a symbol of victory, of power as she escaped looking below at the enraged demons.

Not a second sooner than their feet had left the ground a titanic amount of water emerged.

"I'm ready!" Bow replied to Raven.

Raven and Bow held one another's hands firmer and finally the usual current of electricity that ran through them sparked. Visualising the two city centres overlapping they managed to push the mental images into place. To allow for the mass amount of water, they briefly slanted the city at a slight angle, the floods headed down stream to a huge whirlpool at the end of Abingdon Road. The demons screamed as they were sucked into the sewage of the real city centre, being left eternally to wade through the under-city swamp.

"Punk, get the humans out!" Raven commanded.

Running back down the very long staircase of the Sheldonian, Punk headed to the doors to release his makeshift belt lock, "RUN!" he screamed at them.

Still petrified they did as their saviour asked.

Raven and Bow's hands repelled thrusting them to either side of the library room they had been sat. The dimensions parted and the demon's trap detonated. The humans stood outside of the real Sheldonian confused and with no memory as they had crossed the barrier back to reality.

Zen and Ash soared onto the roof of the real Bodleian Library, slowing down into a jog with River.

Now normalness was restored and realising that Bow's makeshift megaphone had disappeared, they all took out their phones; one text was sent amongst the group.

'The Grapes'.

* * *

"So how did your wings work – I mean aren't they magick?" Guy inquired enjoying a pint with his corporeal hands.

"What do you mean? Someone actually expected they might not have worked?" River wondered desperately.

"Well there was a moment of doubt in the back of my mind, how about you Ash?" Zen teased.

"They worked because they are part of them, they may have been made with magick but the roots were always inside. And I don't think the demon dimension was entirely magick proof – if it was then we couldn't have all spoken to one another," Raven explained.

"Oh well, another day's hard work done, let's hope the next mission is something a little less taxing," Ash commented.

"Tell me about it," Bow laughed.

Beware of the Gnomes

'Dear Mr and Mrs Lane,

I am writing to you as your loyal and cheerful companion of, I believe, fifteen years in this lovely sunny front garden on Cricket Road. I am not complaining about my lodgings at all. Benny the cat has been very obliging and often fetches me treats. However, I feel that you no longer enjoy my company and so I am enquiring whether you feel I should move to another location or perhaps enjoy a holiday. My dear gnome friends tell me a holiday can be a lovely experience, and of course I would delight in sending you a postcard.

I understand that as humans you find it hard to understand gnome communication but I am of course able to understand you. If you would care to instruct me on your wishes for my future I would be most grateful.

Best wishes,

Derrick.'

"Can you believe it? I'm not quite sure whether to see the funny side of it or be worried. Of course, years ago Nan and I would have laughed and accepted it as a harmless joke from one of the neighbours, but nowadays you just don't know. To be honest darling we're a little worried," Frederick explained to his granddaughter Rena in their weekly phone call.

"I'm sure it's harmless, probably some kids messing about. It's nothing to worry about. I need to go now, but give me a call soon. Hey - perhaps cook Derrick a bacon sarnie!"

"Well you know what your Auntie Kaz had to say?" Frederick said holding on to the phone call a little longer.

"Go on," Rena prompted.

"She said to 'get him some eff-ing friends.'"

Rena laughed, "He can chill with his Gnomies then!"

"Yes, well, maybe that's it then. I shall want some gnome friends as gifts when I see you next time. I will inform all the family, Uncle Edward, Auntie Lynn, the lot of them!"

"I'll inform the cousins, I'm sure Nan will be happy about a gnome invasion! Bye Granddad!"

"Bye Darlin'," said Frederick. He put down the phone and placed it on the placemat in front of him at the head of the dining table. He picked up the note and looked at his wife who was sitting opposite him.

"I shall keep this to show Edward, Reet," he said.

"Yes, well I heard you talking about getting more of those bloody ugly monsters, if it wants to go on holiday then you bloody let it, it can bugger off. I heard the dump was nice this time of year," Reet joked as she slowly walked into the kitchen with a duster and polish. She placed them down on the side. As usual, in the day, the back door was open. Reet looked out into the tidy back garden as she lit her cigarette sitting at the small kitchen table with a cup of tea and a rich tea biscuit.

Frederick was still sat at the large table in the front room looking through the net curtain thinking it would be nice to have a couple more. "Perhaps we could move him to the back; he does seem a little neglected out there on his own," he said to himself.

"What the...?" Reet shouted in her smoker's voice, as she looked up from dunking her biscuit, "Fred, Frederick! There's another one of those bleeding things in the garden, did you put it there?"

"I've been sat 'ere on the phone, what do you mean there's another?" Frederick shouted through to her, confused. He slowly got up and walked into the kitchen.

"Well I never, where 'as that appeared from?" he quizzed.

"Someone's having a laugh with us aren't they?" Reet answered.

"Well, maybe we should keep it," Fred suggested. Reet didn't say anything.

The day passed in the normal fashion of the Lane's household. Reet was reminded by her neat note on the dining table, that the bins were being collected the next morning. She stepped down carefully into the back garden.

'That's funny,' she thought as she noticed the newly appeared gnome from earlier that day. It had moved from the washing line to the step on the patio. "You creepy thing, I know where you can go," she picked up the laughing gnome, which was holding a cup of tea, and placed it in the wheelie bin.

With no more thought about it, the Lanes went to bed after their usual tipples: a Martini and lemonade with a packet of ready salted crisps for Reet and a whiskey followed by a few lagers for Fred.

The next morning, Reet was down first as usual, making the breakfast whilst Frederick spoke to the family on the phone.

"That's funny Fred, postman's early!" Reet picked up a note from the mat, which again was just addressed to 'The Lanes'.

'Dear Mr and Mrs Lane,

We are deeply offended by your reaction to our last letter and wish to tell you that this is a formal declaration of war on the people of Oxford. Now you will come to understand the power an army of gnomes possesses. Please inform your city's leaders.

Yours sincerely,

Derrick and Rodger on behalf of the Gnomes of Oxford.'

The Lanes were quite shaken. The joke, if it was such, was no longer funny.

* * *

It wasn't just the Lanes who were taken by surprise: Oxford was under siege. Gnomes had left their owners' gardens and made their way into the city centre overnight. An army of gnomes circled the window ledges of the Radcliffe Camera, others stood back to back on the Bridge of Sighs. In fact, every available ledge of Oxford's noble architecture had been invaded by gnomes. The local paper's headline read:

'IT'S GNOME LAUGHING MATTER AS CITY WAKES!'

Followed by a brief article:

'Today the residents of Oxford have been woken up to a fleet of grinning ceramic ornaments that have been placed around the city centre. Some people have speculated it is part of a mass student project whilst others wonder if it has a more serious message – just what are the gnomes trying to tell us? The city council is in debate whether to leave the welcoming ornaments up or whether the joke has run its course and it is time for the rosy-

cheeked fellows to go gnome! Commuters have offered mixed responses; "I think it's nice, whoever did it; it's attracted a lot of attention and become a conversation piece." Abbey Smith, student of Hertford College said. Others haven't given the gnomes such a welcoming reception, "Oh, they're hideous, creepy things, I think. I'll be glad to see the back of them."Josh Hart, senior employee of the Central Library commented. The gnomes seem particularly popular with the elderly, some students and parents with very young children. Even if they don't stay with us for long today their presence will certainly be a memorable welcome to the city centre.'

* * *

"Hey, have you seen this?" Bow said carrying the paper as she walked into Punk's place with Raven.

"Yeh, a mate from uni' just rang me, pretty cool huh?" Punk replied relocking the many bolts on his door.

"We should go and get our photos taken with them before they are taken down," Raven suggested.

"Shall I round up the gang?" Punk enquired.

A loud knock at his door interrupted them.

"Hey, shouldn't you two be asleep?" Punk greeted Ash and Zen.

"Yeah, well there's a problem," Zen said.

"Want a cup of tea?" Punk offered as he finished locking the door's bolts once again.

"No, no, no, no, no, no tea, no wellies, watering cans, pointy hats, any of that is the last thing I want," Ash said.

"Not keen on the gnomes, guys?" Bow joked.

"Gnomes that sit and do as they're told - no problem, gnomes that plot to slaughter the city, they kind of put me off the whole package!" Ash informed.

"Looks like we won't be having that photo after all, but still better round everyone up," Raven said, sighing.

"I'll alert River," Punk said and hit 'call' on his mobile.

"Won't she have already seen?" Bow wondered.

"No, she was working out of the centre last night, patrolling the graveyards on the outskirts," Ash filled in Bow.

"She'll be happy then," Bow joked.

They all sat waiting for the slayer to appear, wondering just how one defeats killer gnomes.

* * *

"We should wait until tonight; I really find it hard to believe an army of pottery pests are going to slaughter the city. Guy is keeping an eye on things for now," River said, reassuring Ash who was really wound up about them.

"I think it's cute. Not many people have a gnome phobia," Zen said, kissing Ash's hand, trying to stop him from pacing up and down Punk's apartment.

"Babe you heard them too, you saw them talking!" Ash pleaded.

"Yeah I did but they're gnomes, not really scary," Zen reassured.

"It's got to be a spell, I've searched all my books and I can't find anything that details crazy psycho gnomes," Punk declared.

"What if they're not gnomes, what if it's some sort of shape-shifter?" Raven wondered.

"Nah, it can't be, people recognised their own gnomes," Bow reminded him.

"Well there might be a stash of gnomes somewhere; it could just be imitating the ones it has seen," Zen joked.

"A gnome graveyard, jeesh," Ash started pacing the apartment again.

They spent the day looking through Punk's books to double check there was nothing they might have missed. Guy said that things in the centre were normal and it looked as though the council and university were allowing the gnomes to stay temporarily. As soon as the sun set they were all on their way to investigate Zen and Ash's claims of the gnome's evil plot.

"You know you're going to get pulled carrying that axe," River kept informing Ash as they marched up St Aldates nearing the police station.

"Well, I'm sure Bow can use her hypnosis if that's the case, the axe makes me feel safe," Ash said defensively.

"What if they're indestructible chaps?" Guy questioned, having now joined the group.

"Oh, trust me, one way or another, they'll be destructible," Ash declared.

A gusty breeze picked up around the city, and as the group reached Radcliffe Square it was apparent the breeze wasn't nature's doing. Gnomes were swirling around like out of control helicopters, they should have been smashing but something was behind their power. The gnomes spun mid-air around the Radcliffe Camera where they started losing formation and re-moulded as part of a greater huger being; one colossal gnome - larger than the Radcliffe Camera itself.

"Are you kidding me? See I told you they were plotting something," Ash said.

"Let me tell you something Ash, gnomes cannot do that. Raven was right; it's a shape-shifter - some sort of lost energy that seems to be taking the form of gnomes to obviously transform itself," Bow concluded.

Ash sprinted at the huge smirking creature, he struck his axe in its leg but the pottery was too thick. It kicked Ash into the wall of All Souls College.

"Any ideas," River asked.

"Raven and I need to get somewhere we can

concentrate to take this down Riv'. But by the time we do that, it will have destroyed the city," Bow said.

"Excuse me old chap, sorry for asking, but my friends and I were just wondering what business you intend in the city?" Guy shouted up.

"Yeah, that'll work, talk it to death," Punk mumbled.

"I AM VESH, DARK SPIRIT OF THIS CITY AND MY SLUMBER HAS BEEN DISTURBED," the colossal gnome didn't seem so friendly with its roaring voice echoing out from its hollow body.

"That figures, how much you wanna bet that Vestra is behind this, she can't do magick so she'll release a stroppy evil spirit instead," Bow muttered.

"Well nice to meet you old chap, I'm Guy. So remind me again, how do you intend to spend your time here?" Guy continued.

"I SHALL DESTROY THIS LAND AND ALL THAT IS IN IT."

"Friendly chap, don't you think?" Guy added to his friends.

"We can't let him do that, Riv'," Zen stated the obvious.

"Why not? You know if this poor lost, nowhere-to-go dude wants to destroy the city, then let him. Raven may have been right earlier," Punk winked at River and chucked her a small box from his back pocket.

"Guys, you catching the drift?" River checked.

They all nodded now understanding what Guy had started.

The giant gnome didn't like being mocked at all. In his brainless anger he took a giant swing at the Radcliffe Camera, his arm shattered and the disturbed spirit was released to the sky. Bow and Raven guided the spirit into the small box which River held open. She snapped shut the box once the grey gust had been pulled into it like a magnet. To finish, Bow and Raven sealed the box with more incantations and magick. The body of the gnome fell backwards smashing on the cobbles of Radcliffe Square.

"Well, I had wished the next mission would be easier. Perhaps I should make a wish more often!" River joked.

"So, now the hard work presents itself - clear the mess up and find the real gnomes!" Zen said.

"Can we forget that last part – and just let people find them themselves?" Ash asked.

Everyone laughed.

"Excuse me sir, I want you to drop your weapon and turn around very carefully," a voice said from behind them.

"See, I told you you'd get pulled by the cops," River said smartly.

"Bow, a little help?" Ash asked.

"As long as you find and return all the gnomes to the correct gardens by morning," Bow replied.

"Oh, alright!" Ash moaned.

And so Bow hypnotised the policeman convincing him that he hadn't seen them. Just for extra measure, she intercepted his radio with a false call for help, he left in a hurry. In the end everyone helped locate and return the gnomes, it was a little easier with magick.

"Tonight I'm going to have a lovely sleep and this will all just be like a weird dream," Ash concluded.

"Yeah, that's not a bad idea," River agreed. "Hey, we make a good team, but I guess we could use an extra pair of hands sometimes."

"Hey Riv' – be careful what you wish for, it might just come true!" Raven reminded.

In good keeping with a new tradition, they retired to The Grapes for a quick drink to wind down before last orders were called. From there they would head to their homes where they would wait for the next adventure to reveal itself.

* * *

"Reet, what did I tell you? It seems like it was all a big prank, that gnome business, after all!" Fred shouted through to the kitchen. "It says here, in the paper, that everyone's gnomes have been returned and order restored. Apparently a young lady was behind it all, her name was Vestra, doesn't give a second name. Anyway, she's going to court for the nuisance she's caused."

"Oh," Reet called back taking a drag of her cigarette followed by a sip of tea.

As she looked into her cup, she missed the wink of the laughing gnome standing by the shed in their tidy garden.

Indigenous

Merec, a proud knight of Oxenaforda, walked back into the well camouflaged camp he and his travelling companions had pitched earlier on Shotover Nature Reserve.

"What news do you bring Merec?" Lief, a small, beautiful, short-haired, girl in medieval clothing addressed her lover.

"There is no explanation, the people look the same but they dress and speak differently, they carry apparatus, there are no horses but mechanical cabins that move on wheels with lights, boxes with windows are everywhere and these beings seem to reside in them. We must stay safe in here with our people until we learn what has happened and where we have awoken," Merec explained.

"I shall keep watch then but still do not let our people know that their Night Watchman is a girl, they will blame me, say that we have been cursed on my behalf for taking on a man's role."

A man walked to Merec and Lief carrying a staff, "I have checked the perimeter. I believe my magick will hold off any intruders and continue to cloak our camp; we need to enquire with all our people about their recent behaviour. I suppose we are still in Oxenaforda, I recognise this land, but it is only little which is left of the land we once knew, many structures can be seen surrounding the woodland from over the hill. The year is no longer 1139, of that I am sure," the warlock informed.

"Dearest Quinn, perhaps it is a question of time travel if we are on the same land?" Merec quizzed.

"Perhaps, but let us rest our weary heads tonight and explore the land more thoroughly tomorrow," Quinn replied.

"We shall. Your magick is working adequately here?" Merec asked.

"It seems to be," Quinn said holding onto his staff tightly.

"Perhaps a combination of our skill and magick can help us feed our people tonight?" Merec answered.

"I spotted a couple of deer on my perimeter search earlier and a few birds, there is little meat, but some fruit," Lief informed.

"We shall do our best," Merec reassured to his two best friends.

* * *

"Have you seen this? 'DRAMA GROUP'S SECRET SURPRISE FOR OXFORD?'" Punk showed River the headline.

"No, tell me about it," River replied picking at her cereal.

"Well apparently a few locals spotted a bunch of people dressed in medieval costumes wandering around Shotover Nature Reserve yesterday. The article says that there was more than one sighting and the people were really in character, they apparently even spoke differently and seemed confused. The paper is speculating that it's a drama group doing a street theatre event, you know like a flash mob but acting," Punk explained.

"Hmm, weird. Sounds cool though; wonder if it's just Shotover?" River said.

"Why don't we have a walk later? Round the group up, it's quite overcast out with the rain, I'm sure Ash and Zen would be able to manage a walk without being sun-fried," Punk proposed.

"Sure, give them a call," River said distantly as she recalled her strange prophetic dream last night and feared that what Punk had just read to her was the start of it coming true.

"Hey, you know I'm thinking of charging rent, I can't remember the last night I had this place to myself, and now breakfast," Punk joked as he wrote a group text – it would take too long to ring everyone; especially the ones that liked to talk forever.

He looked up from his phone at River who hadn't fired back a witty comment as usual. "Didn't sleep well, huh?" he asked.

"Huh? Oh. Well, I had a dream, one of those really vivid ones that occasionally actually come to pass," River explained.

"What happened?"

"I'm not sure, but we were fighting to keep time from falling, we were failing though and well it was the start of the end. Every piece of history clashing with the present and then Raven was struck. Bow was crying over him on the ground where his body lay, and then we started weakening. I lost all my strength, you lost your memory,

Guy disappeared, Zen and Ash turned bad, and it was, well – the end."

"Oh," the mood in the room changed.

"You think this nature reserve thing has something to do with your prophecy?" Punk wondered.

"I don't know, but it might not be a bad idea to check in with Brother Oxford. We can go to St Mathew's Church. It's only a ten minute walk at most from here," River felt a little better for having voiced her concerns.

* * *

Zen and Ash lay asleep in the dark bedsit near Paradise Square that River had sorted out for them. She knew the landlord well and he had given her the bedsit on very low rent as a favour for 'scaring away a cluster of troublesome youths' for him once. Little had he known they'd been ravenous vampires! She mainly stayed at Punk's (when she wasn't patrolling) so it made sense to let her vamp allies hang out somewhere that wouldn't require breaking the law to enter. The room was just large enough for a double bed with a small bedside cabinet squashed in next to the wall. There was a little space left in the corner opposite the door for a TV next to the very small shower room. It was perfect for them.

BZZZZ-BZZZZ

"Ignore it," Ash said as Zen turned to grab her phone.

"What if it's a crisis?"

"It's always a crisis. Wouldn't it be nice to just have some time together oblivious to the world and its problems."

"It would be."

"But?"

"But, we'll have an angry slayer knocking at our door if we do," Zen located her mobile, her eyes still shut. She squinted to read the message. "It's from Punk," she said.

"That's just cruel. We've only been asleep a couple of hours, you know there really should be some flexibility for nocturnal folk."

"'Come to mine, nature reserves need checking out. Punk,'" Zen read.

Bow's East Oxford room was quite similar to Zen and Ash's, a lot larger though which was handy for working spells. Bow and Raven were knelt at her altar reciting morning blessings to the Higher Powers. All five elemental candles were lit and a fresh incense burning.

"Blessed be," Bow concluded her prayers. Raven snuffed the candles as Bow thanked Air, Fire, Water, Earth and Spirit, he was careful not to knock her delicate instruments such as her scrying bowl, mirror, crystals, chalices and fresh flowers – a daily offering to the Goddess.

Bow stood up and accepted Raven's arms which were held out ready to embrace her. His white t-shirt was soft and warm; she loved listening to his heart when he hugged her. They could have happily stood together all day, just embraced, in a dream state, recalling their first days together.

"Phone," Raven said softly at the sound of Bow's text alert. He kissed her hair and let her check her message. Taking a cigarette from his back jeans pocket he pulled up the window and leant out to light up.

"Oh, two messages. Both from Punk."

"Might have guessed," Raven laughed.

"First he said the nature reserves need checking, but then changed it to say we need to visit Brother Oxford first."

"Why didn't he just tell us that when we got to his place?"

"Probably to wake Ash and Zen if they'd fallen back to sleep."

"Figures."

"Good job Guy keeps his gadgets when he chooses to lose matter, can you imagine how hard it would be to find him every time something like this happened otherwise," Bow said thoughtfully. "You know, I think Punk had a thing for that astral walker I told you about, Louise. I guess it's a good job she and Blake don't need to play a role in this reality. That would complicate things."

"Punk? Nah can't you tell, he and River have a thing."

"Well if they do they haven't done anything about it, trust me I'd know if my best friend was with someone."

Raven smiled.

"Well I would," Bow defended.

"Watch them; they have definitely got a thing!" Raven teased Bow as they got ready to walk to Punk's place.

* * *

"I'm really glad we're checking in with the boss before hitting the nature reserves. Did I tell you what I heard at Uni?" Punk said as they approached St Mathew's Church.

"Yeah - that some students had a night out never to forget. So? They were probably drunk and stoned," Ash groaned, standing under an umbrella with Zen, protecting themselves from the small chance that any sunlight might penetrate the dark clouds.

"Man, they were not, these kids are ruined, half of them have dropped out of Uni and moved home, the others are having serious counselling," Punk shot back.

"I told you it was seriously haunted at Grandpont," Guy added.

River didn't say anything, she was still somewhat bothered from the nightmare she'd had last night.

"You ok Riv'?" Bow looked at her best friend with concern.

"She just had a bad dream," Punk put his arm around her shoulder, punching her friendlily with his fist, trying to cheer her up.

Raven nudged Bow. Mentally he spoke to her; 'See, told you.'

Bow stuck her tongue out at him.

"Can we just get in here before someone announces the bosses name; it freaks me out when he bellows at us on entry," River finally spoke.

"Sure, Riv," Bow reassured.

They all walked into the church, which fortunately was empty.

"Brother Oxford?" River spoke quietly, weaker than her usual fiery self.

"River, something is on your mind my child," Brother Oxford appeared behind her, placing a skeletal-like hand on her shoulder. River felt calm, not alarmed as she usually did when Brother Oxford appeared.

"I had a dream last night, and then Punk brought the morning's headline to my attention. It was about people of the past being spotted in one of the city's nature reserves. I guess it's freaked me out a little," she explained.

"The dream you had may be prophetic and that we must discuss in detail at a future time. Today, I can reassure that you will find people of the past, but not foes. In fact, they are friends summoned to become your siblings in this sacred order. You must approach them with caution; they will be extremely bewildered at the modern world. Welcome them into the group, use your magick and gifts to help them adapt, when they are ready bring them to me to be initiated. River's dream was not one to ignore. The goodness you all supply will be a burden at times but it will also come with rewards. Your friendship with one another is vital. Now, good luck today. Oh, and go easy on the pub runs, wickedness doesn't wait at your convenience," said Brother Oxford and bowed his head, fading before any further questions could be asked. That or because he knew the Reverend was due to walk into the church.

"Excuse me, the church is closed to visitors today. Perhaps if you would like to come to worship you could return on Sunday for the weekly service?" the Reverend gently asked, a little in surprise having being met by an unexpected group of visitors.

"Sorry Father, the door was unlocked and so we thought the church was open to call into," River replied respectfully.

Everyone smiled politely, quietly exiting the church.

They all stood in Marlborough Road.

"Where do we start?" Raven wondered.

"Closest first, slowly working our way around the city's nature reserves," River decided.

"That means Grandpont, urgh," Punk groaned.

"Wait, you read the article right Punk?" Bow remembered.

"Yeah," he replied.

"So where was the named location?" Bow prompted hopefully.

"Argh I can't remember, let's swing past the newsagent on the corner of Whitehouse Road and check," Punk suggested.

"Phew, I wasn't looking forward to a trip to hell," Guy said through a sigh of relief.

"You know we're going to make you go through there one day, it's not that bad, right Ash?" Zen said as they began to walk towards the shop.

"Yeah, a couple of addicts here and there, the odd troublesome spectre but nothing supernatural like we've already faced, no gnomes, demons, stroppy angels... shall I go on?" Ash mocked.

"So, anyway, what do you think these new siblings will be like?" River said.

The mood livened up again as they realised today could be more positive than they had originally anticipated.

* * *

Quinn opened one eye as he adjusted his position against the tree he'd slept against last night. The sound of a crow alarmed him, he glanced at the camp.

Everyone had gone - everyone but Merec and Lief who were asleep on the dusty mud.

"Oh my!" he whispered under his breath. Alarmed he turned to look behind. There was not a trace that anyone had ever been with them. 'Perhaps we are indeed home and it was but a dream,' he wondered.

He stood shaking the bark of the tree from his silky long hair. For a second he considered taking a walk to peer through the clearing; to check there would be no futuristic establishments waiting, as he'd dreamt. Interrupting his thoughts was a tremendous buzzing, he thought it was the sound of the earth shaking but he did not feel unsteady beneath his feet, perhaps a new species of dragon then? Quinn glanced up witnessing a mechanical structure, flying, how could this be?

"WHAT ON EARTH IS THAT?" Merec shouted over the sound of the low-flying police helicopter. "AND WHERE IS EVERYONE?"

"I WOKE UP AND EVERYONE HAD GONE, I HAD THOUGHT THIS CRAZINESS TO BE A DREAM," Quinn returned.

"WE MUST FLEE - WE'RE NO MATCH FOR THIS CONTRAPTION," Lief proposed.

They all ran, out of the thorn hidden, magick cloaked campsite. Turning right they sprinted through the path amongst the trees until they came to a sudden halt as they stumbled across a group of strangers.

An armed, tall, muscular, short haired man in suede trousers part covered by a long burgundy tunic stood next to a petit lady with blonde cropped hair in a long cloak, also armed. To her other side was a peculiar looking man with aged silvery long hair but a youthful face.

"I think we've found our siblings?" Guy broke the brief silence.

"Looks like it," Ash grinned, accidently exposing his fangs.

"TIS A MONSTER!" Merec shouted gruffly.

Without hesitation the indigenous wizard aimed his staff toward the group of strangers. Lightening like magick burst from the carved tree branch he held. Not particularly wishing to find out what the apparent wizard was capable of Bow and Raven threw their hands forward effortlessly envisioning a shield around the group. The magick bounced away flying past the three indigenous and slicing a young tree in half.

"Hey, easy now," Punk shouted.

"They're frightened," River reminded him.

Merec drew his huge sword brandishing it skilfully; he slowly made his way towards River. She dodged his blows as he swung at her. The knight did not give up however, but River was too good. When he swung his blade low she jumped, when he aimed higher she ducked. He just wasn't giving up so she decided to throw a few karate kicks at him. "You really don't need to attack us you know, if you don't stop you're going to feel my throws," she warned becoming bored of this game.

Zen and Ash circled the three attackers hoping to make them feel threatened and give up their unwelcome aggression. Bow and Raven threw back Quinn's magickal lightening trying to avoid anyone getting hurt.

Guy distracted Lief throwing himself around the small clearing. She fired arrows trying to strike him before he disappeared. "You're pretty good, but you'll never hit me sweetheart," he taunted.

"Riv, watch out," Punk shouted as one of Lief's arrows flew toward her. River dodged it but it was still in Guy's path.

Lief was an excellent archer; however Guy was too fast to hit. Her arrow sprung from the bow with such accuracy, she very nearly pinned Guy to the large tree he stood in front of. As he faded from sight the arrow pierced the bark.

"OUCH!" an unfamiliar nasal voice groaned.

Everyone paused, exchanging looks.

"Is this how Oxford's protectors should choose to greet one another? Really, Brother Oxford will be disappointed to hear of this," the voice continued.

The clear confusion on the strangers' faces made Merec, Lief and Quinn cease their attack.

"Can I just take this opportunity to say that we are not monsters and in fact probably your only friends," Ash slipped into the silence.

"Now, can we continue being confused as to who just spoke?" Punk wondered.

"Back here guys," Guy shouted from behind the tree.

Cautiously everyone walked to where Guy was now standing. Not taking her eyes from the strangers Lief caught her foot on the tree's roots and tripped over, Zen caught her hand breaking her fall.

"Thank you," Lief said quietly.

"Oh ho ho, that tickled," the voice chuckled.

"Well well, a talking tree," Raven commented in wonder.

"Someone has to keep an eye on things around here, now," the tree had a very large crooked nose, two friendly eyes sat snug to it, its mouth was rather small and square but nonetheless friendly looking.

"Merec, Lief, Quinn, you have been called to this time as part of a sacred order to protect the city you once knew as Oxenaforda, it is now known as Oxford. Much has changed and you must learn how to adapt to this new world. You were born to take on this role and you will live eternally – only, however, if you choose to accept this fate."

"And what if we don't?" Merec spoke on behalf of his two friends.

"You will be returned to 1139 where you will fight many more battles, die young and witness much horror," the nasal-toned tree explained with a cheerful tone, despite his words.

"The alternative is you could walk by our side, read about what has happened in your past through our history books and have a wonderful life, as well as fight lots of battles and witness plenty of horror," Bow added sweetly.

"Hey man, can I just ask, did you inspire Geoffrey of Monmouth to write about Merlin?" Ash sincerely asked Quinn.

Quinn returned Ash's question with a confused stare.

"It may not have quite been published in their time Ash, besides they may not be able to read, no offence guys," Punk explained. He turned to the three indigenous, "But if you do decide to join us then we can teach you everything you would ever desire to know, plus I would really love to learn how you wield your sword so skilfully."

"Did we not pray for a better fate just a few nights ago? This is our calling, our chance to have a wonderful future; we would be fools not to take it," Lief persuaded her friends.

Quinn and Merec exchanged a glance.

"Do all the trees talk around here?" Quinn wondered.

"Not to our knowledge," Raven replied.

"By my life, this new land may not be so bad then," Merec decided.

"Welcome to the gang," River held out her hand to Merec.

He shook it firmly bowing his head, "I should apologise for being so quick to attack."

"Don't worry, it's quite understandable. Just, maybe best conceal your blade when we journey home," River advised.

"Merec," Merec introduced himself. "And this is Lief and Quinn, as you may have already gathered."

"I'm sorry too," Lief apologised taking turns to shake hands with her new friends.

"Yes, I regret I could have hurt you," Quinn said.

"Let's not worry. I'm River – Oxford's slayer. This is Punk, my very knowledgeable watcher; Zen and Ash, sort of nice monsters, we shall go into that later; Guy, an adaptable ghost; Bow, as you know a gifted witch; and Raven, forged by the Gods and blessed with much power and many talents," River quickly ran through everyone.

"Mr Tree?" Bow enquired.

"My name is Zephyr actually, Bow. But how may I answer your query?"

"I just want to say thank you, and wondered if you could tell Brother Oxford – however you do that – that we will visit soon when our new siblings have adapted," Bow walked to the side of the tree; avoiding his face she hugged him gently. "I'm really glad to have met you; we should visit you again in the future."

"Well Bow, I'm really glad to have met all of you, I do hope you will visit again," Zephyr replied, he smiled then gently shut his eyes.

"Ok, so are you guys ready for a culture shock?" Zen asked as they began to walk through the woodland.

"Hey, maybe we should spend some time here first, show them our smart phones, a few photos, and then after we've found them a change of clothes we should head to the pub, right?" Guy suggested.

"Yeah, The Grapes sounds good," Ash agreed.

"You know Quinn, your power is really impressive but Bow and I may be able to help you use it from your very finger tips rather than the staff. Merec, Lief, there must be something we can do to enhance your skills too," Raven said cheerfully.

"And we must think of a name for our group now that we have a nice size family!" River said.

Merec, Lief and Quinn all looked at each other. "Well it's always nice to have such a warm welcome on our travels!" Quinn remarked.

"Quinn, don't be silly, you're not on your travels - you're home," Ash patted him on his back.

"Yep, amongst all kinds of friendly monsters," Punk joked.

They all chuckled, as they stopped to sit on some fallen logs.

"Shall we warm things up around here?" Lief asked.

"You ready?" Quinn prompted Raven and Bow. Together they ignited a small camp fire in the centre of the circle around which they spent most of the day sharing tales and getting to know one another. Ten of Oxford's protectors sat celebrating unaware of the burden the future may hold for them.

The Phantom of Oxford

January 2015

Nearly ten years since Zen had taken her first step into the city and left her life behind. Her future waited for her as she had alighted from that bus all those years ago: she would die, rise, fall, and then be bitten. Ten years since River had been made Oxford's slayer. A decade since Bow had realised her powers as a witch. 2015: A special anniversary for the three most dominant female figures protecting the city. They had built on their strength with Ash; Zen's vampiric angel companion and Punk, River's unofficial watcher. Then there was Raven, their power source and soul mate to Bow; Guy, the city's ghostly tour guide. Plus, there was Merec, indigenous knight of Oxford; Quinn, his warlock friend and Leif, the castle night watchwoman – thankful not to have to hide her true gender in this modern century. Guiding them were the Higher Powers, and representing the Powers was Brother Oxford. 'Oxford Alae', they had recently decided to call themselves. Merec told them that it roughly translated to

'Oxford Wings'. It was only just the commencement of eternity for these warriors but they were already strong and wise to the city. A celebration was in order for the upcoming anniversary and tonight they would meet at their favourite local, the Turf Tavern.

Though they usually gathered to drink in the cosy beer garden, Oxford Alae stood out from the other punters. Even in civilian clothing the un-human pallor of their eyes and skin, and the presence of their fangs, for example, was a little difficult to hide. The Turf had a good atmosphere and they were welcome there. Sometimes they would wear cloaks for fun, they attracted a lot of attention on such nights and people usually wanted to take photographs. The bar staff were used to them and if they were suspicious that there might be more to this strange group than just a liking for fancy dress, they were clever enough not to quiz them, it was clear they were not troublemakers.

"You think we're gonna get a lecture from Brother Ox' for taking a break?" Punk wondered.

"Nah, he's sound, and he knows how hard we work usually. It's not like there's going to be anything horrific happening in the next hour," Zen said confidently.

"Well, should there be, it is on your conscience for being a drunkard," Merec added light-heartedly. His hair was a medium-brown shaved very short, he was tall and muscular, pure skin, and rosy cheeks.

River walked through the low door from the bar with a top up ale for Quinn, the long silver haired, youthful looking warlock, and a Bloody Mary for herself.

"How could you forget me?" Ash seemed offended. "You know we can't go inside, with bar mirrors around."

"More to come, be patient vamp!" River snapped back, in good spirit.

"Ash, your lager, and Zen, a WKD," Bow called through following River.

"All topped up now?" River asked.

Everyone nodded as they sipped into their drinks.

"So what did we miss?" Bow enquired, looking affectionately at Raven.

"Punk was being paranoid," Raven filled her in.

"About what?" River enquired.

"Bruv' Ox' getting cranky over us boozing," Ash replied.

"He'll be fine," River replied.

"What could happen tonight that would be so tragic in a matter of a couple of hours?" Bow said certainly.

"That's exactly what I said," said Zen.

"Well, not to be a spoil sport but the amount of things I've seen in my time on these streets, the possibilities are endless," Guy filled in.

"Shut up, Ghosty," Leif piped up. "Let's forget work for two minutes and have some fun."

"A toast!" River proposed.

"To Oxford Alae!" Bow said.

"I'll drink to that," Zen said as they all clunked their bottles and glasses together.

"I can't get my tongue around the Latin," River admitted.

"Ey-lee, it's easy really," Punk offered.

"I still love the meaning, 'wings', it's so broad...taking Oxford under our wings, looking down at the city from heights we could reach with wings, guarding the tower wings of Oxford, and of course it's angelic too," Leif said thoughtfully.

Merec smiled at her, the others thought it was cute how they obviously were in love but would never admit it publically.

Zen and Ash looked at each other cautiously.

"What's the matter?" Raven asked picking up on their nervous tension.

Urgent shrieks prevented Zen and Ash from answering. A girl emerged from St Helen's Passage, blood on her hands and tears streaming down her face, "Please help! My friend's been murdered! Help!" She was breathless in her panic, desperate to find someone to help her in her distress.

The group looked at each other.

"Someone call the police and an ambulance," River shouted towards the bar, "She needs looking after."

"Come on, let's go an' find the body before it gets taken away," Ash suggested.

Beers still nearly full after their toast were left on the benches. Oxford Alae ran towards where the girl had come from and made their way to the body, following the drips of blood to the joining of New College Lane and Queens Lane.

"No bites," Zen noticed as they reached the young male. "Possibly a student?"

"His throat has been sliced," Merec observed moving the head of the victim gently with his leather gloved hand. "It's high, under his jaw."

"I can't believe this has happened right under our noses," Quinn said remorsefully.

"We'll track the weapon," Zen said to Ash.

"This is an unusual death, Quinn, any ideas?" Bow suggested.

"Perhaps a reoccurrence spell. But that will take a few days to prepare," Quinn supposed.

"We'll hit the books instead then, look at historic murders, sacrifices, anything to narrow down the motive," Punk started walking beckoning Bow and Quinn.

"I can ask around, see if any spectres were passing, I reckon it would be too soon for this poor fellow to come back to haunt," Guy added.

"That leaves us three, fancy some roof tops?" River asked Leif and Merec who were standing alone with her.

"Dost thou want to take St Mary's?" Merec asked River.

"Sure, that's a good vantage point. Lief, take the back streets in case the murderer is still lurking, and I'll check the perimeter around the Bodleian," River proposed.

"We're on it Riv'," Leif obeyed, respectful of River's leadership.

The group had dispersed in different directions determined to get to the bottom of what had happened so gruesomely on this cold dark night. In their panic they hadn't noticed the cloaked figure watching over them from the ledge of New College, standing to the right side of the central statue. He carefully climbed down to the ground, heading towards the High Street.

The light from the street lamp revealed his eye mask; blonde shoulder length hair tidily tied back in a black ribbon and his very expensive attire. He looked as though he had walked out of the eighteenth century.

"Going somewhere?" a voice startled the masked man. He turned, drawing a sword.

"No blood. So it wasn't the sword that you used to kill him?" Raven observed. Everyone had been so busy rushing off that no-one, not even Bow or the eavesdropping masked man, had noticed Raven had held back in the shadows.

In a blink, smoke appeared before Raven. He waved his arms through it but the swordsman had disappeared.

* * *

"What do you mean he disappeared?" Ash asked as Raven recalled the incident to the group back at Punk's flat.

"I literally blinked, there was smoke and he'd gone. No trace, not down the road, or on any of the buildings. He just dematerialised. It was as if he was a ghost," Raven explained.

"Could he have hopped over a wall? Got down a drain manhole? Even managed to get through a door?" Punk suggested.

"No man! There was no time, it was a second," Raven said.

Quinn pursed his lips, "Sounds like sorcery. Perhaps it wasn't a straight forward civilian murder after all."

"Oh, please not more bad witches!" Bow said despairingly.

"It could be either right? Either sorcery or he's a ghost," Zen concluded.

"You know guys, it's pretty rare for the ghosts around here to be able to manifest physically, and you know it is only magick that helps me take physical form. Bow is the only witch I know of alive and strong enough to perform such magicks and even so it was with Raven's help that I was given my gift," Guy added.

"You don't suppose Vestra could have reacquired her power?" Bow asked.

"Well if she has then we are all in trouble," River said.

"Vestra?" Leif questioned.

"Nasty jealous witch; used her powers to cause huge mayhem. The Higher Powers - with the help of Bow - stripped her of her magick eventually. That wasn't enough though, so she released a grouchy bad spirit who took the form of a huge garden gnome and tried to destroy the city. She's in jail now. I'd be highly surprised if she could find a way of getting power back, she angered a lot of people!" Punk filled Merec, Quinn and Leif in.

"Yeah and embarrassingly I paid her to help me manifest physically," Guy admitted sheepishly.

"So most likely this phantom dude has a few tricks up his sleeve. I wonder why he didn't hurt you, Raven," Ash said.

"He didn't have any blood on his sword, and I think I startled him. We don't know if he actually did anything, for all he knew I could have been the murderer," Raven considered.

"Well folks, looks like we have the Phantom of Oxford on our hands and possibly a murderer," River wrapped up.

"No boozer for a few nights I suppose then," Ash said sadly.

"And no Bruv' Oxford, I do not fancy a lecture just now," Punk added dryly.

River's mobile rang. "It's Damien," River slid her finger across the screen to answer the call. "Hey D, what's up? Three bodies all with slit throats, damn it. No, we only knew of one. Where were the other two found? St Michael's and St George's? Ok. Let me know if anything comes up. Thanks D."

"Is this personal? Queen's Lane is pretty close to the original city wall, St George's the West Gate and St Michael's, the North Gate," Punk concluded from what he had heard of River's phone conversation.

"That means the next could be Christ Church way, we need to patrol the backstreets near St Aldates," Leif proposed.

"Why Queens Lane, why not Merton Street or Rose Lane for the East Gate? I don't get it," River wondered.

"Perhaps it's a distraction to get us thinking in this pattern," Merec stated.

"Or maybe it's nothing to do with us and we're being paranoid. We need to find out about the victims. The police won't be able to catch the killer if he's supernatural like us," Bow said thoughtfully.

"We're over thinking this. Let's get our heads down tonight and work this out in the morning, I think he's made his or her point for now. What are the chances of something more dramatic happening tonight?" Guy tried to reassure the group.

"And this is coming from someone who was earlier this evening telling us it's quite probable for chaos to unleash whilst we are relaxing?" Zen queried.

"Well I was right then, wasn't I?" Guy smiled.

"True. But if I wake up tomorrow morning to find some dramatic headline like 'Blood painted over stage of the New Theatre!' then I'm going to be really tetchy," River stated.

The small flat on Abingdon Road housing ten sacred protectors that evening was full of fear and dread for the people of Oxford. Bow silently prayed to Itus, God of protection for the innocent. She hoped in her heart that this phantom guy that Raven had seen was one of them as she closed her eyes wearily, the last tired warrior to fall asleep.

* * *

The night was beautiful; especially with vampire vision. The stars looked brighter, the nightingale's song was sharper, and Zen's face was different, different to how Ash had once seen her. He didn't look at her as he once had perceived her. Through his new eyes he now saw her passion for creativity, a craving to thrive in the happiness she had found with him. He hadn't always understood her, but he had always cared about her, even if she hadn't let herself believe it. It was hard when he was a mortal to think on any deep level, he didn't care much if he lived another day... until he fell in love with her. Being a vampire had given Ash a second chance. He had been middle-aged as a human, a big difference to Zen's young years. As a vampire he had lost a decade in appearance, looking more like thirty. His hair black and now styled differently, flat and combed half over one of his eyes, his skin purer with the loss of stubble. The blood intake made him slightly more muscular, able to show off his arms with a tight black t-shirt, just like when he had first met Zen. He completely understood the power Raven radiated; love was a mysterious wonder that had strengthened the group. Ash stood on the roof of the Radcliffe Camera, gazing down wistfully towards Brasenose Lane where he had first learnt Zen's secret. It seemed a lifetime ago. He stared at a couple walking towards Market Street, they looked happy, but Ash had a weird doubt, he observed them carefully. The couple had reached the shadow of Lincoln College, but Ash could see as clear as day. The guy forcefully pushed the girl against the wall near where Zen had thrown Ash to protect him from the demons one night. Ash didn't need to see anymore to decide whether to intervene. Using the magick Raven had enchanted on Ash and Zen, Ash spread his huge black wings which grew on demand. He glided down to where the attack was happening just as the girl screamed.

"Run!" Ash said to the girl as he grabbed the guy by his arm. "I don't allow dirt in this city," Ash's fangs pierced the would-be rapist's jugular, the blood trickled out from the puncture in the vein onto Ash's tongue and soothingly down his throat. So fresh, it was rich, delectable, an evident difference to the animal substitute from the Covered Market butchers. He liked to take his time emptying the life out of scum, making the death slow and agonizing, enjoying every drop. The corpse wilted under Ash's grip as it was drained. Ash dropped it; feeling satisfied he made his way back to Punk's abode.

It was just three in the morning; he'd only needed an hour to sleep off his weariness of trying to track the murderer from earlier in the night.

Zen sat on the roof of Punk's place, waiting for Ash to return, he'd woken before her, obviously thirsty for authentic blood. "I can smell the liquor on your lips boy!" Zen crooned as Ash flew in.

"Then perhaps you should lick it off," Ash teased her. Her lips met with his, his fang scratching her lip, he sucked a little blood from it.

"I take it that wasn't the murderer's blood?" Guy materialised next to them.

"Fffffff..." Ash started.

"...sake," Zen continued.

"What is it with ghosts?" Ash asked.

"Sorry, but you're not the only one that doesn't need as much sleep," Guy explained. "And what is it with vamps and blood and lust, get a room!"

"Well we kind of had a roof until you interrupted!" Zen stated.

"Sorry Guy, I guess you miss that girl, what was her name?" Ash asked.

"Ange, she was beautiful, ginger hair, pale skin, and rosy cheeks. I wish I could have stopped her from leaving. She seemed pretty freaked when she learnt my secret, we were getting so close. She was so interested in all the history I had to tell her; my favourite myth; 'The curse of time' or sometimes known as 'The barrier of time'."

"What's 'The barrier of time'?" Ash enquired.

"Well there is a myth that there is a ritual which can only take place in Oxford, at different locations within the city. If it is performed correctly all the barriers that sequence time and keep it apart will fall and all the eras known since the beginning of humanity in Oxford will merge causing havoc."

Zen looked at Ash and then back to Guy. "And you only thought to tell us that now? You know, with a phantom masked guy and a bunch of murders surfacing?" she said.

"It's only a myth," Guy said.

"So are vampiric angels, powerful witches, a human forged by the Gods, a slayer, a ghost tour guide, need I go on?" Zen ranted.

"Yeah, you kind of have a point there," Guy realised.

"Who's going to wake up the grouchy slayer?" Ash enquired.

Zen and Ash both looked to Guy.

"Oh great," Guy groaned.

* * *

September 2014

In his cloak and mask Jose stood, a shadow behind the large tree at the front of the churchyard, part of the night as the group of five walked past.

"Yeah, let's just worry about the freaky monk for tonight," the human guy said.

He waited until they were all a little way past the vicarage and down the hill heading towards the lock. Cautiously he walked towards the church and entered.

Brother Oxford was waiting for him, his hollow hooded robe visible by candle light in the dark chapel.

"I trust they didn't see you?" the monk enquired.

"No, Brother. Need you ask?" Jose replied.

"Don't underestimate them; you will fight by their side one day."

"They're younger than I expected, modern."

"You'll adjust."

Jose looked at Brother Oxford, "Perhaps."

"How was the journey?" Brother Oxford enquired.

"Rough, but I coped, it's not every day one gets to die in the 18th century and be resuscitated in the 21st."

"No, but I trust the Higher Powers have provided you with all the information you need to adjust?"

"I'm prepared; now let's get this thing done... Unless of course I've been ignorant in my lack of concern for your passage from our last meeting to the present? It has been two or more centuries since we last spoke."

"Indeed it has. Well, the journey was a little rough. I was executed and then they made me a Martyr and now I live eternally between the present and the afterlife. But thank you for your concern. Yes, down to the reason we're here. The scroll is bound in the spine of this book; the book needs to be guarded with your life."

"And what of the children?"

"They are not children, Jose, most are in their twenties and older."

"Yes, but what if we cross paths?"

"In the unlikely event of that occurring, show them your medallion. But they will only have to bear the burden of this task if the scroll is found by those with evil intent."

"And then what?"

"The truth; that the scroll is the recipe for chaos, a methodical ritual detailing the location of four swords, which if struck in the centre of four of the city's clocks will cause the very barriers of time to collapse merging each era of Oxford into another, every being of history alive at the exact time, the present time; causing ultimate mayhem. Only tell them in the case of absolute necessity," Brother Oxford urged.

"I understand," Jose replied.

"Have you thought about accommodation?"

"Tonight the theatre, tomorrow somewhere else."

"Remember you look out of place. Stick to the shadows until you learn how to blend in."

"You don't need to worry," Jose assured.

Brother Oxford picked the heavy book from where it lay on the font of Iffley Church. He passed it confidently to the masked and cloaked man, the Phantom of Oxford, his old friend Jose. They exchanged a strong hug of good will.

Brother Oxford faded; Jose turned his back and made his way out of the church. He followed the ancient hidden tunnels and clung to the shadows to reach the centre of Oxford. On reaching the inside of the New Theatre he slept on the fly floor hidden by the stage's set, it wasn't ideal but it would do for tonight.

* * *

River was pacing the length of Punk's front room.

"And you're sure you know nothing of these scrolls?" she asked Quinn, Merec and Lief for the sixteenth time.

They exchanged a look of blankness.

"I'm gonna kill Guy!" she continued.

"Yeah, except he's already dead," Ash offered.

"Riv, you know I think 'overreacted' may be the wrong word but perhaps if you were a little forgiving for Guy's urgh..." Zen searched for the right word.

"Stupidity," Guy said appearing next to Zen who was perched on the arm of the sofa.

"Seriously? If I wasn't dead too I'd have lost count of the times you'd have given me a heart attack!" Zen shouted at Guy's ghostly manifestation.

"Actually you mean cardiac arrest... and you were just talking about overreactions?" Guy joked back sarcastically; he loved watching a vamp jump. He continued, "Look I'm sorry guys, I just well, you know there are so many myths, I just thought it was one, maybe when this business is done Punk and I can bash our heads together and write a book for our reference. And another thing, there is no evidence of any scrolls detailing the ritual; it could just be passed down by word of mouth. Anyway, something I didn't mention earlier is that one of the swords is supposedly hidden below ground, there's a riddle."

"Don't keep us in suspense!" Bow prompted.

"Ok. I think it goes:

'A century placement on a street,

Beyond the bell of Ye Ol' Tom's call,

If the past ye wish not to meet,

Be it at your peril for time to fall,'" Guy recited, looking to the ceiling as he recalled the words.

"I hate all that poetry gibberish," River replied grumpily.

"If you break it down it will be easy," Merec informed.

Quinn looked happy, "So a century doesn't necessarily mean one hundred years in a riddle, it probably simply means the number one hundred."

Lief continued, "Yes and the second line is easy, it will be opposite the Old Tom Bell."

"So, the next line is simply linking the final, which I believe is a message disguised as the second part to the third line," Merec finished.

"Enlighten us," Ash said bored of all the chatter and lack of fighting.

"It's 'fall', isn't it?" Punk crosschecked aloud.

"Exactly, it means it is lower, so probably underground," Lief agreed.

"So are there tunnels from Christ Church?" Quinn asked.

"No, I know where it is," Bow said.

"I think we're thinking along the same lines, beauty," Raven proposed.

"It's my tattooist, Oxford Tattoo, there's a dungeon under the shop," Bow revealed.

"I know you find the basement spooky Bow but seriously, it's just an old building!" River joked.

"No, no, I sense it every time I go down there; the vision is so strong it is unbearable at times."

"The studio's in the basement?" Guy asked.

"No, stupid, the bathroom," River filled in.

"Ok, but why the tattooist?" Zen wondered.

"100 St Aldates! It's further up the road from the Old Tom, and when you are in the basement the sound of the bell is fainter which makes sense; 'Beyond the bell of Ye Ol' Tom' and 'for time to fall'...it all pieces together! There must be where the sword is hidden!" Bow declared.

"Go tattooed girlfriend!" Raven complimented.

River looked confident in Bow's theory. "How are we going to access it?" she asked.

"Do you think we should be accessing it, is it not safer where it is?" Merec enquired.

"Look how easily we just figured out the riddle. If someone else has access to it and a little bit of logic then..." Punk argued.

"Yeah, he's right, it would be safer with us lot for now," Ash decided.

"Ok, we need to head to the studio," River concluded.

"Remind me how we are going to get in?" Guy asked.

"I'll ask Marc if we can go and have a look, I'll explain why," Bow said, looking at Guy as if he should have already known that.

"Sure, and shall we just go and tell the Town Crier too?" Guy replied churlishly, getting a little tired of being in the dog house even though he had contributed a ton of information... eventually.

"We can trust Marc," Bow replied putting her arm around Guy and giving him an encouraging squeeze.

"And if he doesn't believe us?" Merec queried.

Ash and Zen revealed their fangs, Guy flickered his physical self.

"Good point," Merec realised that the majority of the group had supernatural skills enough to make even the most sceptical believe.

"Ok, so we'll hit the tunnels and meet you near the entrance," Zen said to the others.

Bow looked at the clock, "10:10 A.M. OK we need to get to the shop at the same time as Marc, before the customers start arriving."

"Just don't be disheartened if we're wrong," Lief said softly to the group.

"Let's go," Punk gestured his hand toward the door which would take him five minutes to re-secure to his satisfaction.

River, Bow, Raven, Guy, Lief, Merec and Quinn left Punk's third-floor, large bedsit on Abingdon Road followed by Punk with a huge bunch of keys.

Ash and Zen made their own way and as usual were at the location first and stood waiting in the dark sunless street next to the Old Tom pub. St Aldates was quite quiet for the time of day.

"10:40, not bad considering Punk took so long to get out of the house!" River teased.

"Ok, let's do this," Raven said, holding Bow's hand securely.

Screams, once again interrupted the group's conversation. A well-dressed woman stood shrieking and shaking on the opposite side of the road. Soon it was obvious what was causing her distress. A bloody body lay across the entrance of Blue Boar Street.

River held her breath instead of letting out her frustration, how could this have happened under their noses.

"We're on it!" Punk said, looking at Lief, Merec and Quinn. They ran over the road.

Raven looked up and once again spotted the masked figure. "Hey guys, Town Hall!" he shouted.

"Go, we'll be ok," Bow said to him. He hesitated but then decided to help the others, letting go of Bow's hand unwillingly, he joined them running across the road, then up the side steps of the building trying to chase the masked and cloaked, 'Phantom of Oxford.'

"Let's not waste any more time," River said.

Ash, Zen, River, Bow and Guy entered the parlour and approached Marc who was standing with a book in his hand to the side of the counter, obviously disturbed from the sharp shrieks and commotion outside a couple of seconds earlier.

"Hi Bow, what can I do for you?"

"How much time can you spare?" Bow replied trying to figure out the sanest way of explaining the request in hand.

"See, told you he'd be cool," Bow said to Ash, Zen, River and Guy a few minutes later as they followed her past the desk, through the heavy white door and down the stone curved staircase. The basement was dark, cold and spooky. Bow had always thought it was haunted. She looked behind her at Guy, "Sense anything?" she said.

"Er, Bow?" Ash interrupted as she had failed to notice what they were all staring at.

Bow turned to look, and halted in her steps. The entire back wall of Oxford Tattoo's basement was gone. In its place were jail bars – like you would expect to see in a medieval tower. The gate in the bars to the 'dungeon cell' was open.

"Damn it. How could someone have got here before us?" Bow cursed.

"What about that masked dude, he was here, right? It's gotta be him," Ash concluded.

"No, wait, look, there's another door in there," Zen noticed as she walked forward inspecting the space.

Sure enough in the small cell of about fourteen foot square, there was a hidden door in an alcove of the right hand wall.

"Come on, let's go," River said marching past the others who were hovering by the bars cautiously.

They looked at one another. "Looks like the sword has been taken, unless it wasn't actually here," Guy put in.

"It was here," Ash pointed to a sword-shaped disturbance on the dusty cell bench.

"Well, no use hanging around an empty dungeon. Come on, let's go and find out where the door leads to," Zen said.

One by one they walked through the old wooden door and found themselves in a long tunnel. The stone floor was damp, drips were falling from the arched ceiling; darkness surrounded them. They walked through steeling themselves to be brave for whatever might be greeting them the other side of this tunnel.

"I can hardly see," Bow said.

"Here, have my lighter," Ash pulled it out his jeans pocket.

"What about your magick?" Guy asked.

"I fear if I use it down here it will drain me, so I'm kind of at a disadvantage not having slayer sense, or ghost or vampire sight," Bow replied.

For the first time that River, Bow or Guy had noticed, Ash and Zen were holding hands, a trait of their humanity. It was quite sweet, both were confident, cool vamps but nevertheless they could not live without one-another and their fear revealed this. Zen walked in front, her hand held in Ash's who was close behind her, towering over her by half a foot in height.

"Where do you think this tunnel is going to lead us?" River asked.

"There's a rumour of a stream that flows under the city called 'Trill Mill'," Ash replied.

"It's not a rumour, it exists, and I've seen photos online," Bow corrected.

"If you'd be so kind to let me get a word in edgeways," Guy said through a cough. "I could tell you that Trill Mill starts in the meadows of Christ Church and flows under the city west to, I believe, the outskirts of the castle. I would guess, approximately to the stream which flows to the rear of St George's Tower."

"Right, so you think we're headed towards water, and will probably end up somewhere we could have reached on foot," River concluded.

"Precisely," Guy said.

"Urgh, I think this is our stop," Zen said as she looked ahead at the dead end of the tunnel, a locked old rusty metal door with a steering wheel mechanism as a handle prevented them from going any further.

"Stand back," Bow warned.

With a little of Bow's concentration the wheel spun and the door released.

"Sorted," Ash said starting to walk forwards confidently further into the underground routes of the city.

"Hang on," Bow stopped him. She once again closed her eyes; with her hands she traced the shape of a long crescent. A punt appeared on the other side of the door floating on the deep murky water.

"See, a bit of confidence never hurt, how could your mass of power be drained?" River knocked Bow encouragingly with her elbow.

Bow smiled.

Guy and Ash took turns punting the boat, although Guy had the advantage being non-corporeal on demand he could avoid the low ceilings, so he punted the most.

The tunnel was dark, and the water was deep. When they spoke their voices echoed around the tunnel. Candles had been left lit around ledges of the rounded walls. They noticed many metal loops with ropes attached.

"Someone's been here before us, there are mooring sites, candles lit, someone left in a hurry," Zen said.

"Look there are foot stirrups leading to a manhole, do you think they went that way?" Guy pointed out.

"No, I can feel the heat from more candles, keep going," Ash commented with caution in his tone.

The boat slowly floated under the city. The atmosphere was intense, it was cold and there was poor visibility. There was a severe sense of loneliness surrounding the air despite being together.

"See – more candles," Ash noticed breaking the silence.

"Yeah, I wondered how you could feel heat from just one," Guy realised looking at a host of candles on a larger ledge.

"Wait, Guy, punt us closer," Zen's keen eye picked up on a detail from amongst the candles as she stood up to examine the ledge from the middle of the stream.

"Another sword is missing, that's two. Damn, damn, damn it!" River shouted. Her cursing echoed through the tunnel startling them all. The sword shaped break in the moss of the ledge revealed that they were losing a battle to preserve the barriers of time in Oxford from falling.

"I don't get it," Bow interrupted thoughtfully, "I thought the riddle was supposed to be detailing the locations of scrolls, not the actual swords."

"Perhaps the scrolls have already been taken and I guess we've just been lucky, or well unlucky in the grand scheme of things," Zen supposed.

"Or like I said, there were never any scrolls and word of mouth alone led seekers to the location of the swords," Guy added.

"I think we need to head back to the others," River decided.

"Urm, maybe head forwards, I sort of closed the wall in the tattooists," Bow admitted.

"Better watch the witch when she's deep in thought," Ash joked.

"Right, Guy, get us out of here," River instructed. They followed the stream out, reaching a sealed off end, Bow after all had to use her magick once more transporting them all out to the basement of Oxford Tattoo. They walked up the stairs back into the reception area, a good hour since they had entered, one by one nodding to Marc who looked a little confused having been down in the basement himself a couple of times and not seeing a trace of them.

"Thanks Marc, see you soon," Bow said, leaving last and closing the front door of the parlour carefully.

Punk, Raven, Leif, Quinn and Merec were sat at the bus stop to the front of the studio waiting for the remaining five to return. As Bow walked out, Raven approached her, his arms embraced her. Like Ash and Zen, Bow and Raven did not cope well away from each other.

"So...?" Punk asked.

"How do we summarise this? Let's see, two swords gone, no scrolls, a secret tunnel in the back of Oxford Tattoo which leads to Trill Mill - a secret stream that flows beneath the city, no luck in relocating either the swords or the person who took them," River said through a sigh.

"Looks like it's time to get grilled by Brother Oxford," Ash finished.

"Well, maybe not. We couldn't keep up with the masked dude but he dropped this," Raven took an envelope from his back pocket.

"We thought maybe it's a map, or the scrolls, but naturally we wanted to wait for you to return," Merec explained.

"Well. We're here," River smiled.

Raven handed the envelope to Bow. It was cream parchment, sealed with wax and stamped with a 'J'. She carefully tore the paper from the seal then pulled out the matching parchment from the envelope.

"Oxford Alae, I am not your enemy, perhaps you would be good enough to meet me; tonight if you will, the hour of nine, on the castle mound. Yours truthfully, Jose," Bow read the letter written in beautifully scribed calligraphy which the Phantom of Oxford had dropped.

"So it seems our journey continues tonight," Leif said.

"Indeed it does," Quinn agreed.

* * *

It was the hour of nine o'clock, the eighteenth of January 2015. At the top of Oxford Castle's mound stood a very powerful young witch, next to her an ancient warlock. Strongly placed to his shoulder holding an axe was a female vampiric angel hand in hand with her vampiric angel companion wielding a sword. Half way around the circle back to back with the young witch was the slayer waiting with just her strength and skill. Both holding weapons also were the slayer's watcher and the power source of the group. Completing the circle stood a ghost, a knight and a castle night watchwoman. They were waiting composed, cautious and ready for a potential battle.

"You do realise you look pretty obvious stood at that vantage point?" came a voice from somewhere behind them. They turned and saw a figure leaning against the tree sheltered from the moonlight.

"Come out where we can see you," River ordered, still keeping her position tightly in the circle.

The figure walked forward, a man, dressed in the clothes of a wealthy individual from the old world, masked and cloaked. His hair was tied back with a ribbon.

"Thank you for coming," he said.

"Why should we trust you?" Punk asked.

"Because I am one of you, let's say I'm like your big brother," the man replied.

"How so?" Merec interrogated.

"Had you had the guts to have visited Brother Oxford and admitted your slip from duty during your drunken mingling on the night of the first murder, then you'd be more the wiser. I am a further member called to Oxford Alae. In fact you could say I am the founding member, though I suppose the three indigenous may refute that fact. The point is we're amidst a bit of a screw up, wouldn't you agree?" the man asked. He stepped slightly more into the moonlight, his medallion glimmered.

"Look, I have a thousand questions. Some I expect even in an eternity I will not find the answers to, but I wish to know why you have been running away from us. Why haven't you approached us before now?" River asked.

"I was supposed to be your guardian, guardian of the guardians, but I reason that it's not going to quite work like that. Look, let's not waste time in debate," he presented his medallion to the group, lifting it into clearer sight. "My name is Jose; I was born in 1789. I was induced by magick into a sleep. Brother Oxford has left me in charge of the sacred book in which the Secrets of Oxford are detailed.

There is a scroll hidden in the spine which contains a recipe for the apocalypse, or as you know it 'the myth of the barriers of time'. I have recently discovered this scroll is a copy, someone must have stolen the original when it was written and so we are nearly out of time to stop the barriers of time being broken. We must find and destroy the swords," Jose explained.

Oxford Alae, who were not long ago stood tightly shoulder-to-shoulder were now scattered facing, listening to the masked man.

"So there were no scrolls at the locations, just the swords?" Guy enquired.

"That is correct to my knowledge. Although the truth is unclear, some believe each sword sits with a scroll which tells the seeker of the next location but others say the swords are alone and it is for the seeker to work out the rest. Though that doesn't matter anymore, whilst you rested today the third out of four has been stolen from beneath your very feet, from the depths of the well in the mound. I left for here as soon as I had dropped you the note earlier. I tried to stop the woman but she was gone and some wretched man called me into the castle where I was expected to tell money givers the history of the area," Jose complained.

Punk laughed, "They thought you were a tour guide, kind of amusing."

"Yes, but what isn't amusing is that we have goodness knows how long until chaos hits the streets again," Bow broke the lighter mood.

"We must work out where the last location is," Ash realised.

"The first three swords have been below ground, the tattoo parlour basement, Trill Mill, the midst of the mound, there must be a pattern," Zen said in a stressed tone.

"You must also know the swords must be struck into four towers, not clocks as one rumour suggested. The towers are St George's, Carfax, St Michael's and St Mary's," Jose added.

"I'd wage a bet that the fourth sword is near St Mary's," Quinn rubbed the slight stubble on his face.

"The Radcliffe Camera, I'll bet!" Lief guessed.

"Sorry to interrupt the brainstorming but you said it was a woman who took the sword this morning?" Guy enquired.

"Yes," Jose answered.

"Describe her," Guy demanded.

"Orange hair, slim, not that tall, pale, a few freckles," Jose returned.

"Ange," Guy whispered, weakly.

"Don't worry bruv, you weren't to know," Ash patted Guy's now corporeal back.

Jose thought about asking more about the connection, but decided he had a good idea already.

"There's one last detail. Time is of the essence. The towers can only be struck tonight, and they must be struck all at the same time, this 'Ange' cannot be working alone. We will know when the spell is active as all the bells of all the three out of four towers will ring in unison," Jose rushed.

"Oh, you mean a little like that?" Raven piped up, holding Bow close to him now.

No sound had ever been heard like it, the sound of the bells awoke panic as they all rang fiercely. Time in Oxford was going to mean nothing and soon chaos would arise.

"You know as much as I love Oxford, I'm getting a little irritated with the towers," River moaned.

"It's started," Merec stated.

"Indeed it has," Brother Oxford appeared before them all on the mound.

"Now we're in the dog house," Zen observed.

"How did you...?" Guy wondered.

"With the barriers of time gone I am free to walk," Brother Oxford replied. "Oh, and yes Zen, good observation, you rather much are. If we get through this mess and I ever catch you drinking when you're supposed to be on duty then I will curse you in a way which alcohol will literally be your poison. Are we all quite understood?"

The group nodded. Brother Oxford turned to Jose, "Now, let's show these 'kids' how we do things."

"Wait a minute – now that we're all coming out in the open, can I take this opportunity to ask who the murder victims were that Jose always seemed to be around?" Punk enquired.

"Spies," Jose answered.

"You were being spied on by recruits of the movement that has unleashed this pandemonium," Brother Oxford added.

"And you killed them?" River interrogated Jose.

"No, they were killed by their own, to frame me. They knew I was in turn spying on them and when you lot were around they pulled their gruesome stunts," Jose defended.

"Right, now we've cleared that up and are all friends can we deal with the chaos that is surrounding us, for instance the archers that are currently aiming this way," Bow pointed out.

"Oh great, how are we going to ever stop this, surely there's no going back now that the past is bleeding into the present?" Zen grumbled.

"Listen very carefully, we have a window, we have time. At the moment those from the past aren't quite real, they're flickering between realities. They can't yet hurt us, or anyone else for that matter. Soon you will have prisoners of many eras suffocating for lack of space in the dungeons. You will have medieval guards beheading prison guards of HMS Oxford Prison. Goodness knows what in the city centre; sixteenth century peasants browsing twenty-first century department stores - and as for the roads – Victorian stagecoaches colliding with the modern local bus services. Imagine a current family dining at their table to be disturbed by the many families that had once lived in that very house. The headless horseman's execution will be witnessed by church and college goers. Not to mention the live stake-burning of the Martyrs on Broad Street. Soon there will be plenty of hangings from which medical students will try to steal the bodies. Townspeople of 1355 will be rioting against students. The brutal end of the civil war will be fought as King Charles escapes. Toilet pits shall be emptied onto Jewish graves which are to be dug all in the same location and at the same time as the Botanic Gardens are being created. It will be a disaster. Current animal rights protestors will be faced with the crisis of bear-baiting on Alfred Street. All this is just human history, imagine centuries of vampires, werewolves and demons causing havoc on top of the violent history of Oxford. We must stop this now, we need to split up and take the city back in time. Whilst the swords are mounted into the roofs of the towers the clocks can be changed back. Once the three clocks have been taken back, you may remove the swords, time will rewind and no-one will be the wiser. Does everyone follow?" Brother Oxford instructed very clearly.

"What about Ange's people – how do we stop them? Surely they will guard the towers?" Guy enquired.

"The people who struck the towers must be sacrificed," Jose bowed his head to the floor with a hint of regret in his voice.

"You mention three towers, what must be done about St George's, there is no clock?" Ash asked.

"Clever lad, you will be met by a guard; he or she will be disguised as a knight but will be holding a sand timer. You must smash it," Brother Oxford explained.

"And how do you know all this?" Punk asked suspiciously.

"Prophecy!" Brother Oxford and Jose said in unison.

"Well you might have warned us," Punk said awkwardly.

"Right, listen up; I vote Lief because she is familiar with the castle layout, Merec for his might and Jose for skill to take St George's. For Carfax: Zen you're the strength; Quinn you can use your magick to reset the clock, Guy you'll use your knowledge to help them. Bow I want you to use your magick on St Mary's, Brother Oxford is very wise to the ways around the church. Ash, I want you to defend them. Finally, Raven you'll work your powers on St

Michael's. Punk is our encyclopaedia and extra strength as with it being a narrow tower I may need extra muscle to ascend if they if they attack from above. Is that ok with everyone?" River prepped.

"Good mapping River, just remember clocks first then swords. We have a small space of time for the swords to be removed and clocks rewound. Do not let your conscience spare any blood, four sacrifices of the evil who initiated this is a small price to pay for the many lives that could be destroyed once this is irreversible. Beware of the past. Now everyone go," Jose shouted.

Merec drew his swords from the neat sheath tied to his belt as he ran with Lief and Jose.

"You two reach the tower from inside I shall meet you up at the top," Jose instructed as he took a leap from the stone slabs on the ground onto the wall, grasping the cell bars and beginning his climb like a pro. His cloak was flying as he swerved the ghostly arrows being shot at him – he wasn't going to take a chance of them 'flickering between realities'. With an almighty blow Merec shattered the glass front to the Visitors Centre of the castle making his way through with Lief. Guards were already attempting to execute them. Some were able to run through walls like ghosts, others would bounce off as they temporarily became flesh.

Bow had taken one each of Ash and Brother Oxford's hands transporting them inside the chapel of St Mary's with her magick. "Ash, you will be at a disadvantage if they know you're a vampire, you may need that sword to disarm them of crosses. Brother, try and defend any throws of Holy Water against Ash – I trust it won't burn you?" Bow asked.

"It won't Bow, I shall do my best. As you know the climb to the tower is extremely steep, it is claustrophobic; there will not be much room to swing your sword. There is a landing where the bells are rung, if we are attacked try to bring them down there. You will also have the same issue of lack-of-space at the top. I suggest we split up. Bow you will need to be standing directly above the clock. I shall guard the entrance to the stair case and Ash you can slaughter the bad guy!"

"Wow, Brother Oxford, you're pretty cool!" Ash concluded.

Quinn too had managed to transport his team to Carfax Tower.

"Ok, I'm gonna re-set the clock, I'm counting on you two to distract the enemy. Guy how's that corporeality working for you? Bounce around, get them to chase you. Zen you take the kill," Quinn decided.

"Quinn you're going to have a problem," Guy said worryingly.

"What are you talking about?" Zen wondered.

"The clock used to be on St Martin's Church which stood in front of the tower, if the past is flickering then who knows where the clock will be," Guy warned.

"I shall stand on the corner of the crossroads – on the High Street. Do you two think you can get to the tower without getting hurt?" Quinn questioned.

"Yes, but I think we should all take the sword out, will you transport yourself to the tower when you have rewound the clock?" Zen said running towards the 21st century door in the hope of not being knocked out by a large church threatening to reappear.

"I shall. Good luck," Quinn shouted.

River, Punk and Raven had only just made it to St Michael's. River wanted to put her trust in an alternative route. She had Raven fix the flickering illusion of the original castle wall still for them – it took an incredible amount of magick to make this possible without it destroying the present buildings that stood in its way. In fact it was only really possible to create a bridge like pathway using the surface of the original city wall, the stone structure beneath flashed to and from sight. Punk - with good knowledge of the original wall - shouted the directions from behind so they would not fall to the ground before the path ahead appeared. They ran. They jumped over towers, dodged soldiers as they appeared before them. It was exhilarating. Having reached St Michael's tower River and Punk started fighting off the opposition. Raven stood directly above the clock, then leant himself over the wall focusing on the hands. A hooded figure was waiting, hanging onto the rim of the tower. Viciously he grabbed Raven's wrist, tossing him over the tower.

"River!" Raven shouted.

"Oh no, Punk, this is it, this is the dream I had!" River ran reaching over the tower to grasp Raven's hand.

The hooded man swung towards Raven, also clutching on. Like an angry mule he kicked back hard, Raven lost his grip, he began to fall. The fall was broken before he had really begun to descend, looking up to see why, Raven noticed Punk had his jacket collar.

"Take our hands!" Punk ordered. River and Punk tugged Raven as he climbed back onto the tower. But not before a blow to his back with a huge blade wielded by his hooded attacker. River and Punk pulled him over. He collapsed on the floor of the tower, bleeding.

"Give me that dagger," River shouted at Punk.

She had to use her strength before it started to weaken due to Raven's injury.

As she caught the knife she raised her arm throwing it down immediately in the might of her fist. Slam! The dagger sliced taking the attackers fingers clean off. He hurtled to the ground.

River chucked the dagger back to Punk and bent down to check Raven.

"I feel fine," Raven reassured them, sitting up.

"Let me check your injury," River looked at the slice in Raven's jacket. The cut had healed.

"Forged by the Gods, remember," he smiled standing, and quickly leant over the clock to re-set it whilst River resumed defending the tower.

Trying to move the hand required much concentration and strength. Without physically touching the hand Quinn mimed the movements, he raised both his arms forward and hurled the magick out of his hands, pulling down on the clock hand he levitated as his weight hung from the stubborn mechanism. Despite being metres away Quinn may as well have been standing on the face of the clock as his magick streamed a solid connection tugging at the time.

"Watch out!" Guy shouted as Zen hurled her axe at an attacker trying to break Quinn's connection. Quinn jolted in mid-air dodging her blade and the clock hand reversed.

"Great, but how are you gonna kill this character now?" Guy said nodding at the hooded cloaked figure holding the sword stuck in the tower.

Zen flashed her fangs as she smiled then pounced, looking forward to a bloody drink. She restrained the sword's guard and hungrily sank her teeth into the appetising vein. The blood trickled faster than any she'd tasted before, emptying the body rapidly. The hood of the sacrifice fell back as Zen sunk her teeth in harder.

"Ange?" Guy croaked weakly, a pain cut through his heart. A pain for the loss of hope and the realisation of the person Ange had been.

Jose had reached the top of St George's. Holding onto the flag pole for support he swung kicking the guy who had his hand held firmly on the grounded sword. Merec made a strike with his own sword sending the sand timer smashing from the 'knight', accidently taking a hand with it. For good measure Jose helped Merec and Lief toss both the faux knight and time keeper sacrifices from the tower.

They hurtled down, their bodies twisting as they met a horrific death on impact with the ground.

Bow, who was charged up with a colossal quantity of magick, succeeded in moving the clock hand of St Mary's back too, a little easier than the trouble Quinn had had. Brother Oxford had kicked a few attackers down the stone staircase – others had run at the sight of a faceless ghost monk. Ash had cornered the sacrifices at the far balcony of the tower and at Bow's blessing had enjoyed their blood.

"Raven, how are you doing?" River asked.

"Done," Raven replied, like Bow he'd found moving time a little easier than Quinn, perhaps the closer proximity had helped.

Punk thrust his dagger into the last evil heart, sacrificing the final body.

River looked over her shoulder as she carefully tried to fight off characters of the past who, not realising the full horror of what was happening, were trying to defend St Michael's tower. She called out, "Ok, on my count, you ready, when I say go we're all going to..."

"PULL!" River, Merec, Zen and Ash instructed their teams.

The swords flew out much easier than any of Oxford Alae had expected, throwing them all against the tower walls.

Like rewinding a film the flickering atmosphere of colliding times began to disappear. The chaos had been worse than the group had anticipated, but all the images of the past – pickings of each century – luckily were just ghosts. For it wasn't just the trouble of people colliding but the re-enactment of fires, of buildings being demolished on the sites of the present day ones and some reappearing. The purpose of each land clashed, university scholars of many eras had re-appeared beside current ones, the Old Radcliffe Hospital was raised from demolition again and with it the many staff and patients. The very first humans were faced with a glimpse of thousands of years of civilisation and its technology. War planes had flown over the city and dinosaurs' roars could be heard. A couple of the monarchs were present in the castle and the university buildings. Every single spec of time had been battling to exist. Fortunately as each aspect grew fainter so did the memory that the boundaries of time had collapsed.

Then darkness.

* * *

"So here's to our strength as a group and the fact that the city is still standing," River toasted. Oxford Alae stood in the beer garden of the Chequers on The High.

"Alas this is not all," Merec announced.

"Spill then," Ash insisted.

"I heard someone has scribed stories of our existence, our role, everything we've done," Merec told.

"A book?" Punk wondered.

"Indeed, 'Secrets of Oxford,'" Merec continued.

"What must we do?" Lief panicked.

"Nothing," River said casually before she knocked back a good chug of her cider.

"Let people believe, even if they doubt, let them feel reassured that there is hope, not everything is black and white," Bow continued.

"How do you suppose the author knows?" Zen asked.

Before anyone actually could suppose, Jose walked through the alley to join the group.

"Good evening," he greeted. In his hand he clasped a small brown sketch book, he smiled rather smugly.

Bow thought, either the Higher Powers had sent a message to someone or Brother Oxford and Jose had a trusted source and the recognition was a 'thank you'. Either way it didn't matter. All that mattered was Oxford Alae would exist for eternity keeping Oxford shielded from anything supernatural that tried to attack.

"So Brother Oxford has dealt with the swords, right?" River checked with Jose.

"So I believe," he replied.

"Are you going to be sticking around with us then Jose?" Raven asked.

"Yeah, looks like it. Besides – someone has to keep an eye on you kids. You know Brother Oxford was not joking when he said he'd make alcohol your poison."

"Well on that note drink up, time for a sweep round the city guys," Zen prompted.

"Our beautiful city," Ash smiled, pouting at her.

So next time you walk through the city have a look around, glance at the roof tops, observe places which look as though doors should be there. Be curious of the purpose of the many underground tunnels. Watch even the air, you might just catch a glimpse or get a feeling that someone's got your back.

Aura Willow

About the Author

Aura Willow lives in Oxford. She believes in vampires, ghosts, werewolves and all things supernatural. Aside from writing she has many hobbies including playing the guitar and drums and getting tattooed.

Secrets of Oxford is her first book but she is currently working on a novel and regularly posts to her Oxford based blog.

If you have enjoyed this book and would like to know more about the blog and new projects please log on to:

www.thesecretsofoxford.blogspot.co.uk

To follow:

@SecretsOfOxford

@Aura_Willow

@SecretsOfOxBook

www.ingramcontent.com/pod-product-compliance
Lightning Source LLC
Chambersburg PA
CBHW051411170626
46809CB00006B/2120